Diane Langford was born in New Zealand and moved to England in 1963, since when she has been active in the trade union, women's liberation and anti-racist movements. Her first novel, *Shame About the Street*, is also published by Serpent's Tail.

Also by Diane Langford and published by Serpent's Tail

Shame About the Street

Left For Dead

Diane Langford

Library of Congress Catalog Card Number: 98–86412

A catalogue record for this book is available from the British Library on request

The right of Diane Langford to be identified as the author of this work has been asserted by her in accordance with the Copyright, Designs and Patents Act 1988

Copyright © 1999 Diane Langford

First published in 1999 by Serpent's Tail, 4 Blackstock Mews, London N4
website: www.serpentstail.com

Typeset in Caslon by Intype London Ltd
Printed in Great Britain by Mackays of Chatham, plc

10 9 8 7 6 5 4 3 2 1

For Brenda Ellis

Acknowledgements

Patsy and Brisons Veor trustees; Centerprise
Literature Project; Anne Darroch; Frankie Green;
Hackney Heckler; Claudia Manchanda; Yaminahtu
Manchanda; Dr Alice Miller & her publishers,
Virago and Suhrkamp; Julia Pascal; Annie
Pfeffercorn; John Williams

'Our capacity to resist has nothing to do with our intelligence but with the degree of access to our true self. Indeed, intelligence is capable of innumerable rationalisations when it comes to adaptation.'

For Your Own Good,
Alice Miller

one

SNOOPING'S A NICE LITTLE earner. Not shit pay and not shit work. Time to stand and stare. And time is money. Right now I'm outside a row of greystone houses behind the High Road, not far from the local Conservative Club. The no-hopers who live in the greyest and grungiest, Widdecombe Hall, have dumped carrier bags full of chicken bones, fish heads and pizza crusts by the steps leading up to the front door. Cats have torn the bags apart, scattering the contents for other urban wildlife to scavenge.

A flock of pigeons have procured themselves a nice little gaff up in the roof. The last few nights I've watched them take turns, pecking away, two perched on the eaves, keeping lookout like a couple of pros. Finally, a slate dislodges and goes clattering down, leaving a gap for them to gain entry.

Down by the messy steps a buggy built for twins lies broken and grown over with convulvulus. All that's left of a discarded umbrella is lifted by a sudden breeze and slaps the side of the house in an angry fit.

Unaware of me, watching from behind my wheel across the street, a woman lumbers down the steps holding her belly as if she's about to drop a bundle. She goes over and starts yanking the buggy from its nest of stringy vines, shaking it out and dragging it up the steps leaving a trail of garbage. Not much to get excited about. After sitting in the car half the night I'm cream crackered, my legs are stiff and my backside aches.

And it isn't over yet. I have to wait and see who comes out. Suspects are using the place like a hotel. *Sans papiers*. Coming here to sleep and making themselves scarce during the day. Working without proper documentation.

A meter maid's eyeing up my motor, dying to jump the gun. Lucky for me, I know the rules. Parking restrictions don't start for another ten minutes. No way is this woman gonna screw things up. I've got mug shots to match with mugs. A little list to compile. But the officious cow's hovering by my car scribbling on a clipboard and blocking my view of the house. So I roll down my window and call out nicely.

'Hey, d' y'mind? I'm on official business.'

Displayed on my windscreen there's an exemption note signed in person by my boss, Gwendoline Rhodes. I point to it, getting a kick out of using the little bit of power delegated to me all the way down from the mighty Gwendoline.

'This don't mean nothing to me,' the woman growls, squinting at Gwendoline's signature. 'I'm traffic police. Nothing to do with the council. You're illegally parked. You got two minutes to move.'

She's busy writing.

'But it ain't nine o'clock yet!'

'OK lady, you asked for it!' She reaches over, picks up my windscreen wiper daintily, stuffs a ticket behind it and lets it spring back against the glass with a loud thwack. While this is happening another figure's hovering on the pavement. I've got a fucking audience peering in through my car window!

Big, cheesy face pressing against the glass. Hair parted

in the middle, pulled back in a bun. Cheeky cow's banging on my window.

'Hey, I wanna talk to you. What's going on? You said you lost your baby!'

Her great tub's rubbing up against my door. Covering my face with one hand, I start the car. Move off slowly. Don't want anyone getting hurt.

'Hey you!' she's shrieking. 'I know who you are, you're a fucking grass!'

She manages to land a few blows on top of the car as I manoeuvre past, then her screams follow me down the road. The parking attendant's waving her fist. People are looking and I sort of duck my head. Just what I fucking don't want. People looking.

Bitch took me by surprise, doing her laundry in the basement while I was in for a chat with the warden. All hours of the morning and she's doing her fucking laundry! Bad luck, or what? Either these people are getting smarter or I'm getting careless. Quick thinking was called for. And I covered up well. The minute she appeared in the doorway with her pile of shitty nappies on her arm, I put my head in my hands and started moaning.

"Scuse me, I saw the light on?' The voice was bossy antipodean-like, demanding an answer to some kind of question. But Sally, the warden, caught my drift and played along with me as I snuffled into the arm of her stinky cardy.

'This is M-M-Mary,' she told the woman. 'She's moving out this morning. Mary's in a bit of a state, aren't you love?'

'Wah! I lost my baby,' I wailed. When I come out with this stuff about losing a baby, Sally dunno where to put herself. Thought I was OTT. Well, I had to cover myself, didn't I? Otherwise, what am I doing in a mother and baby hostel? No baby and no bun in the oven? All hours of the morning? Not bad for spur-of-the-minute thinking.

Cheeseface waddles off and me and Sally go 'phew!', slam the door and pour ourselves a couple of stiff whiskeys.

'God, is she having twins, or what?'

'Had, Montse, had.'

'Whaddya mean? Had?'

'She's already had 'em. It's just that she ain't got her figure back yet.'

'Cor! Don't hold your breath.'

At the time, we both laughed our heads off. Now I'm wondering how much the nosy cow heard while I was having my hooh-hah with the meter maid. Did she hear me say I work for the council?

A few years ago I sign on the dole straight from school. Dealing a little bit of this and a little bit of that, thinking something else'll turn up. They start getting heavy down the dole office. Always sending me on job interviews. And then – work experience. Painting white lines along the edge of tube train platforms was the idea they came up with for my first work experience. When I complain to my youth training supervisor about claustrophobia I get transferred to a gang of blokes scrubbing the sides of tower blocks.

Ever since I was a kid I had falling dreams. Falling out of aeroplanes, off cliffs, down mineshafts, out windows. Always waking in a cold sweat just before hitting the ground. Hanging twelve storeys up in a decorator's cage with a bunch of morons who get off on rocking my cradle and I'm desperate. The falling dreams go into megadrive.

So it's back to the job centre and the same old run-around of restart interviews till finally I'm referred to the joyless, luckless club, the Job Club. Up the reeking staircase where disillusioned job clubbers crouch for a smoke; window ledges covered in rings of dried coffee and green bacteria, stairs strewn with cigarette butts and flattened beer cans.

The place has recently been contracted out yet again. Our host today is Ron who tells us, in the course of conversation, how he once worked for British Aerospace.

'This here's a club and we all are members,' says Ron, 'all in the club. I know it's sorta, you know, ironical, that I'm here, doing this, in work like, because you all are unemployed. I know that. Youse know better than I do how bad things are out there in the real world. But we all have to live in the real world and it ain't easy.'

His wife, Lisa, is the brains of the family. 'Only thirty and she's driving a Porsche,' he boasts. 'You should see the way she dresses.'

'Big shoulder pads?'

'You've put yer finger on it, Montse. And, in retrospect of that, that brings me to networking. Networking is a very helpful way of finding a job.'

Ron networked with Lisa to land the job of leader of the Job Club after she set up a little company called Lisaron.

'CVs are important. And your specutive letter. Do you all know your specutive letter? Paper! Paper is very important. When you're writing your specutive letters don't use paper with holes and don't use paper with lines.'

Ron draws two holes on the side of a giant flip chart and sketches out a few lines to drive home his point, then flips the sheet over. All this is more than flesh and blood can stand. Every kind of creep is coagulated in the Job Club. If you don't attend they cut your dole.

After a couple of weeks I take Ron aside.

'Hey, Ron, what are my chances of getting on the enterprise scheme?'

'Sweetheart, I hate to be the one to tell you, but the enterprise scheme no longer exists as such. That stopped yonks ago. What we have now is a company called Semtec. Run by a mate of the wife's as it happen.'

'Along the same lines, is it?'

'Strickly speaking, it's not within my frame, sweetheart. What kind of business was you thinking of starting up?'

'I heard of people, friends of friends y'know, got on the scheme as clowns, undertakers, you name it.'

'I'm not a miracle worker, sweetheart.'

'How about private detective?'

He stares at his clipboard, then whispers, glancing all about.

'As it happen, I might be able to help you out. In your case, you might not even have to go through Semtec. See, the council are on the look out for people like you. They've asked us to keep an eye. Young, head screwed on. Know what I mean? Leave it with me, sweetheart.'

A few phone calls later and I'm in. Everyone's happy. Ron gets credit for reducing his client list and I'm out of the clutches of the social. Against all odds, the housing department recruits me, little Montse Letkin, as an investigator. Turns out I've got a flair for it.

The council saves grands using me and others like me to do its dirty work. It's a piece of piss for them to recruit a few of us smart ones from the slag heap and get them to spy on poor buggers who still owe poll tax from years back. I don't enjoy dobbing in dole bludgers or harassing poor cows who are co-habiting. Not that I'm in the business of dobbing in mates. I'd never grass up a mate. As far as I'm concerned, with the year 2000 staring us in the face, the whole world is already fucked. No one of my generation can survive with their integrity intact, and I'm talking survival here, not a living death up some fucking tree or burrowing under the latest bypass.

First day at work they give us an induction tour. All round the famous overspend town hall, done up like a fucking great cuckoo clock. Then we all stand in a corridor listening to historical highlights in the ups and downs of the Labour group. Our guide, a woman redeployed from a defunct library, dramatically points to a spot on the lino,

'This is where they met while the Tories fixed a rate in the Chamber.

'It was the first time since 1601 that the right of local authorities to set their own rates had been taken away.'

Then she gives us one of those we-are-the-masters-now smirks.

'Er, just waiting for a few stragglers,' our guide says, 'as soon as we've got everybody with us we'll adjourn to the hospitality suite where you'll meet the Director of Housing, Gwendoline Rhodes. Some of you may have heard Gwendoline's name from the newspapers or television but there's no need to be nervous. Just be yourself if she speaks to you. Chat normally, just as you would to a normal person.'

What is normal? I'm dying to ask.

Out of the ten or so of us who were being inducted, I was the only one actually starting work that very day. Others had been on the payroll as long as three months and were already clued up. One geezer from the engineering works department kept up an alternative running commentary. Stan the Man had worked in other boroughs and thought he'd seen it all. Short, stocky bloke. Black, bushy eyebrows. Pepper and salt hair. Dolled up in a suit for the occasion.

'Let me just run through,' the guide says, herding us briskly. 'We'll be covering health and safety . . .'

Stan interjects. 'Well, that's a load of bull,' he says, trotting alongside her. 'Talk about health and safety. Fucking fire doors won't open and they won't give us the money to fix them!'

In the hospitality suite we loll about in comfortable chairs admiring the fixtures and fittings, except Stan the Man. He's pricing everything and comparing the total to his allotted budget. Our guide unveils a large TV monitor and we have to sit through a crap video of people being nice to the public in the one-stop shop and happy old folk in bright sheltered housing. Titters all round. When we realise it's on a loop and we're gonna have to watch the whole thing all over again, our titters turn to groans. The morning wears on and still no Gwendoline.

'Here, *tempus fugit* mate, *tempus fugit*,' the engineer complains and taps his watch.

'Very well,' the inductor says. 'I can see tempers are fraying. We'll break now for refreshments.'

Coffee is served on a long table covered with thick white linen. While we stand around nervously, Stan keeps us entertained with his Gwendoline stories.

According to him, Gwendoline graduates from some poncy university way back in the mists of time and she makes a beeline for Fords, Dagenham.

'They had a huge car plant out there,' Stan explains. 'Her scam is, get a job on the production line, mingle with the masses, sort their act out for them and get to be their leader. The personnel office at Fords are well impressed. She's got a degree. They offer her work all right. But not on the production line. In management! Very far-sighted of them when you think about it. Because that's where she eventually ends up. But not at Fords.'

'Stan, sorry mate. I don't get it. Why would she want to work in a factory? She's white, she's a member of the overclass and she's got a degree?'

'This was way before your time, Miss, er Nutkin. She belonged to some tiny group of headbangers. International blahdy blah socialists. Infiltrated the Labour Party. That's what people like her used to do back then. Petit bourgeois gits!'

According to Stan, poor Gwendoline cries and shrieks, begging Fords to put her to toil on the production line. It's then, I suppose, when they see the state of her that they twig her game. They turn round and call their heavies to throw her out.

'It was all over the *Evening Standard*, fucking barrels of ink was used up on her, *barrels* of it!' Stan explodes. 'Red Gwen, that's what the papers used to call her. Some people have still got their feet stuck in the past. You can hear them in the pub of an evening, chuntering on about the magnificent exploits of "Red Gwen". Gwen, red! What a sick joke! Their little world ended in the 1970s.'

He's right. It ain't cool to be no leftie any more, lefties went out with Routemasters and red phone boxes thanks to the bullshit artists formerly known as Her Majesty's Loyal Opposition, now HMG.

But that was then, this is now. Gwendoline adapted. She learnt to swim with the tide and bend with the wind. A survivor. Red Gwen became New Labour Gwendoline the Pendulum. But she didn't swing far enough. Since the election she's waited in vain by the telephone while business tycoons and bankers took the jobs she had earmarked for herself.

All I'm worried about on that first day is how to behave if she speaks to me? I decide to keep it light. Not try too hard to create an impression. People like Gwendoline don't like brown nosers.

Then the double doors at the end of the room suddenly spring open and in she glides, moving across the carpet like she's on castors. We all spontaneously form a reception line. Even Stan falls silent. Bunch of prats, biting lips, chewing moustaches, all twitches and tics. And when she gets to me she pauses, 'And you are?'

'Montse. Montse Letkin.'

Ugh! She holds out a froggy hand that makes me shiver slightly to touch it. So boneless it is, so moist and cold. For a minute I can't remember. Who's Prime Minister? Tweedledum or Tweedledee, bullshite or bull crap? If she asks me anything intelligent, I'm lost. Quickly, she smiles and, for a second, the skin's drawn so tightly over her cheekbones, I'm frightened it's going to split.

'My door's always open.'

Her eyes, lit up like runway beams, are full on me. Her spicy perfume which under different circumstances might spark off one of my massive sneezing fits, only adds to the hypnotic effect. Stunned, I realise her irresistible power to charm as well as to chill.

'A bright young person like yourself can go a long way in this organisation Ms Letkin. If you show promise and loyalty, we'll give you a Rolls Royce training. We'll make sure you achieve your full potential. You'll become a highly marketable commodity in your own right. And if you have any problems which you feel your line manager cannot deal with, bring them to me.'

Naturally, I nod. Without further ado she turns her magic beam onto the entire room and launchs into a recital of the council's famous 'no-frills' mission statement, believed to be her own creation.

'No one entitled to housing or benefits will go without, regardless of race, ethnic background, gender, sexual orientation, colour, creed, religion, ability or class.'

Wow! It sounded so good. I was excited when I thought how I'd enjoy telling my mother about my new job.

'There's a ring fence around this borough and everyone inside it is protected. But *only* if they are entitled. Others will be dealt with according to the law. This is the only fair way to do things.

'We don't want to get hooked on wrangles over legality. Always remember. Work strictly within the letter of the law. If you have doubts, check with me before proceeding.

'Our objective is to preserve existing service provision, safeguarding the quality of life of the majority. Every individual in this borough has the option of scrolling through a menu of high quality services. When the phone rings in our one-stop shop it must be answered on the second ring or, I, personally will want to know why.

'We all have to make some unpleasant decisions if we're going to keep within our spending limits. I hope all of you will be able to cope with that.'

Our silence seemed meaningful at the time, but before we had time to work out why, Gwendoline had moved on to the next thing.

'Always remember, our mission is to protect the quality of life of the majority of our customers!

'Finally, it's my very great pleasure to share some wonderful news!' Like an evangelist spreading the good word, she flung her arms open. 'Let you new people be the first to hear of it. I have just learnt that from now on we are going to be able to compete with other boroughs in cross-boundary tendering. Now, I'm sure everyone here understands CCT, compulsory competitive tendering. When CCT first emerged we were all very apprehensive. How would it work? Would it improve our services, or would it be a costly disaster? Well, we were saddled with it. But we made it work for us. The same will be the case with cross-boundary tendering. We can let it be a burden or we can grasp it as an opportunity to shine up our services and display their excellence in the wider marketplace, across the whole metropolitan area or even further afield.

'Remember your SWOT, Strengths, Weaknesses, Opportunities, Threats.'

She spent a few moments dealing with each of the headings.

'Take Ms Letkin's particular field of work as an example. Would it not make more sense for her to operate in an environment where she is not known to anyone? Similarly, we could bring in teams of tenancy relations officers from other boroughs to carry out specific tasks on our patch.'

The engineer was getting in a lather, muttering something about the policing of a long-forgotten miners' strike. Unobtrusively, I detached myself from his group and moved over by the coffee urn. I imbibed all that old left stuff at my mother's knee. How the government sent the Met up north, but what's the point? I'd've been a mug to associate myself with a dissident on my first day at work.

'Anti-social behaviour is endemic in all parts of the country,' Gwendoline told us. 'It's not just a metropolitan issue.'

Councils are the biggest landlords in the country and, all over the gaff, people have got scams going on. Maybe the powers that be will send me to a nice rural setting. Rubbing shoulders with fruit pickers perhaps? No road protests please! Too much like hard work. I'm a city girl, me, but I wouldn't say no to a nice spell in the country.

I was incey last time I went beyond the metropolitan boundary for more than a day. So chubby I could see my own cheeks sticking out. Mum had hired a country cottage for a study weekend and I was left to wander at will in the garden while she and her comrades discussed *The Role of the Individual in History* and *The Part Played by Labour in the Transition from Ape to Man*, that's 'labour' as in 'work', not 'party'.

The birds in the countryside were big as cats and startled me by flinging themselves into the bushes making loud violent noises, or dashing themselves against the waterpipe behind the cottage where they'd go to bathe in the drain. The bees were so loud the noise got on my wick. I imagined a motor racing track nearby with little action men buzzing round in drag cars. Hours after, when I recognised the bee-like quality to the sound for what it was – bees, irritation turned to delight. How lovely it was, to be in the countryside!

Modestly, I let it be known around the council that I had a couple of science credits – total bulldust – but they look at me closer, with more respect, knowing nothing of what the school psychiatrist had told me.

'You're a young woman suffering from deep underlying depression, but you refuse to acknowledge that you are depressed. You are constantly but unconsciously performing attention-seeking acts to distract from your depression. This accounts for your disruptive, anti-social behaviour. You will never be able to pass examinations and you will never be able to hold down a job. You'll be forced to live on your wits for the rest of your life.'

So? What's wrong with living on your wits? And how would he know whether I was depressed? That's a load of crap. I'm not depressed. I'm sorted!

Soon my bosses at the council are sending me on special training courses. Our instructors initiate us into a brave new world. How to place bugs and debug, how to use cameras that see in the dark and how to use jiggers which can open any but the most impenetrable door. I have become a perfect specimen of investing in human resources and flexibility in the labour market. Few are called, fewer chosen. Before long, I've passed my probationary period and I'm on the proper payroll.

As predicted, I became upwardly mobile by living on

my wits. That was the only thing the school psychiatrist got right. He was the one who couldn't hang on to his job. Soon after his crystal ball gazing on my behalf he was made redundant. While here I am, earning money that sad old loser could only dream of.

two

MY FLAT'S A PERFECT little space for one. Not that I'm one of those who calls herself 'one'. Gwendoline calls herself 'one', while others prefer She-who-must-be-obeyed, Great She-Elephant, High Priestess or Dragon Lady.

The way I feel about this place is how I imagine being in love, smitten with hot and cold running water, cable TV, gleaming kitchen and cosy bathroom. Windows and doors flush into walls, ashtray sunk into the arm of my leather sofa. Hell, I deserved a break, but I don't take it for granted. The dump I squatted froze your tits off in winter.

Wallowing up to the neck in a tub full of fragrant bubbles, relaxed and looking forward to vegging out for the evening, I hear the answerphone making noises. Bloke's voice I don't know from Adam, recording a long, rambling message. Why doesn't he leave a number for me to call back? Whoever he is, pillock's disturbing my peace. Poking the towel between my toes, I hear his disembodied voice droning on.

'This is Hughie. Friend of your mam's. She's in the Royal Free. Nothing to worry. It wasn't her idea to phone. It was mine. She wasn't even going to tell you. I've taken it upon myself 'cause she's gonna be in there for a week or more. She might appreciate the support, y'know? That's what I thought anyway. Aw right?'

But my evening's planned! Ricki Lake. Dinner. Few cans and a spliff.

How many mothers voluntarily confess to the crime of not possessing a maternal instinct? Mine's proud of it. Owns up to neglecting me when I was a kid, no problem. It was OK, according to her, because she neglected me in favour of the struggle against imperialism and patriarchy. No faffing around in the Labour Party for *her*! When you put it like that, it's irrefutable; a kid comes a long way down the list of priorities.

Of course, her mind was on higher things. There's lots to consider when you're mobilising the masses to smash the state machine. Leaflets, demos, meetings. Endless. And all for nought. All her crazy rushing around came to nothing. The British road to socialism was a *cul de sac*.

But does she have to dine out on stories of how she left me outside a supermarket and went home, childless, on the bus? Her then current boyfriend, not my father but, I think, the one after my father, asked her, 'Where's the baby?'

'What fucking baby? Jeeesus!' She sprinted all the way back to Safeways where a claque of old dears was gathered around my pram clucking, 'What kind of woman can the mother be, leaving a tiny defenceless babe out in the freezing cold!'

Hard to believe Gwendoline and my Mum belong to the same species let alone the same generation. My mother looks miles older because, unlike Gwendoline, who conspicuously spends a fortune on skin, clothes, therapist, exercise guru and the rest of it, my mother's got a face like a U2 map of Utah. Hair hanging down like spaniel's ears, streaked with grey, and her wardrobe's an uncoordinated mess. Last time I saw her we had this massive row. Silly moi, I thought she'd be pleased I'd got a job at last. Wasn't dealing no more. But oh, no. She starts cussing and yelling like I'm the lowest piece of shite.

'You've gone and bought into the whole rotten system. How could it happen? My own daughter? Where did I go wrong?'

Then I heard she was shacked up with a new man. P'raps this very guy, Hughie. When I say 'new man', that is, 'new' in the sense of *different*. Despite, or maybe because of, her old left/anarchist blahdy blah, my mother never went in for new men of the reconstructed variety.

Anyhow, instead of vegging out on my World of Leather sofa, I'm acting on Hughie's message, tentatively threading my way towards the Royal Free Hospital.

Since our latest big bust-up all my positive moves towards the old tart have received a knock-back. But what if? What if there's something dire wrong with her? What then? Illness, death, and the spectre of things never changing between me and my mum?

Negotiating the familiar streets, I'm in no hurry. For me, driving a half-decent motor's still a buzz. Eventually, passing the point of no return, I'm fixed on my path to the hospital. At a corner flower stall I buy two bouquets. The big pollen-filled one for my mother was a mistake. I'm sneezing before I even make it to the confined space of the car. The smaller bunch is for a dead actress.

Up the top of Church Row there's an obscure graveyard where both Kay Kendall and Joan Collins' mum lie buried, Kay's headstone rickety and moss-covered. Whenever I'm in the area, I bring flowers as a mark of respect for the excellent way she played the trumpet in *Genevieve*.

Sneezing and streaming I'm forced to jettison the flowers, distributing them between Kay and poor Mrs

Collins who lies in the corner with that bastard Gaitskell. When my mother brought me to this dank spot she spat on his tomb. I was shocked! Back then I was shocked because I didn't know dick shit. Mum's unexpected expectoration taught me one thing: you have to know your history if you want to have an opinion about anything in this life. And I do want an opinion. Once a week I sit in the library and read. Hard graft. When I begin I can't get past the first paragraph. Have to pummel my brain, do mental work-outs to improve my concentration. Every day I try to learn a new word. No matter how difficult, I press on to the end of each page, acquiring information from our house to Bauhaus, from aardvark to zymurgy.

My generation's the first to be more ignorant than our parents. Once I read that I made a conscious decision there and then not to be bulldozed into that ditch.

'Education leads to expectations which cannot be met,' said the article, *'resulting in an upturn of psychosocial disorders.'*

School psychiatrists eat your hearts out! Fee education for all! Shut down the schools for a classless society!

Knowledge keeps things in perspective. Couple of facts: 100 companies rule the world, five genes determine the whole of human difference. Knowing stuff like that keeps you from going nuts.

Hospitals freak me out. Can't watch shows like Casualty or ER. Sweet-faced kid cycling between hedgerows. Roar of motor. Drunk driver bowling along in his sports car. Kid. Bike. Car. Thud. Cut to scalpel. Knife going in. Blood spurting. Argh! Hospitals freak me out.

Bossy nurse points me in the right direction. What's going on? Mum's bed is screened. Grey flannel turn-ups with black slip-ons, lisle stockings in sensible footwear, hang down under the curtains. Low, concerned voices conversing.

I sit nearby. An emaciated old woman in a thin hospital gown, clutching a bag attached to a catheter, comes shuffling painfully up the ward. Coming towards me. I hate hospitals and I hate sick people. I'm watching her progress hoping she ain't gonna speak to me. So she stops right in front of me. Drops a copy of the *Sun* onto my lap. I sneeze.

'Here, you can read this while you're waiting to see your mother,' she says. Scottish accent.

'Thank you very much.'

Charming! On the front page there's a baby with two heads and inside a rat with an ear stuck on its back. *An ear, cultivated in a laboratory dish from human gene material, was sutured on to a rat's back.*

The lug that dare not squeak its name.

'Here's your paper back, ta.'

'I haven't peed for two years.'

'Oh?'

'I get an excruciating pain when my bladder's full. That's why I've got this bag.'

'Nice. Got the shoes to match?'

'Cheeky wee devil! Here, see that old girl in the second bed down? Ninety-five years old and can't stop peeing. Doesn't know how lucky she is. I'm lying here in the middle of the night listening to her tinkling away into her bedpan, that's when the nurse makes it on time, and I'm lying here thinking, "Christ awmighty, if only it was me."'

A nurse is lifting a tiny figure with balls of white string for hair, moving her from bed to chair.

'Clasp your hands behind my neck. That's it, Margaret. Give me a great big cuddle. Now let's do a little dance. One, two three hup!' And Margaret is chortling with pleasure, making sounds like a baby laughing. Jesus, if I was getting paid for this I'd charge quids for sitting here.

Now Margaret's upright in her chair and I see a nasty red patch like a stigmata on her temple. She swivels her powerful blue eyes in my direction. 'I itched it' she shouts defiantly, as if she knows I've been looking. From her voice, I'd say, a Galway woman.

Mum doesn't even know I'm here, taking all this in. At least it'll give us something to talk about. Make a change from our usual ructions.

'Come on, Margaret,' nursie wheedles, 'let's get you nice and continent.'

'See?' the bag lady shouts, 'bloody marvellous isn't it.' Then she adds nastily, 'Give her her beads and she can say her prayers for the night.'

Suddenly panicked, I've got to escape. If I get away now Mum will never know I've been here. Halfway down the ward the curtains swish apart and Mum's revealed sitting on the side of the bed, fully dressed while the doctor writes up her notes and hangs them on a hook on the foot of the bed. There's a funny looking geezer sitting on an armchair, holding Mum's hand.

She's spotted me. 'Who the hell let her in?' she says to the geezer. 'I thought I told you I didn't want her coming in here.'

'Mum, what's going on? What are you doing in here with all these old crones? At least let me get you moved to a private ward.'

The bloke gets up. Fat with thin blondish hair. Stubbly jowls. Miles younger than Mum. He's wearing a Queer as Fuck t-shirt. Now what's she into!

'Hi, I'm Hughie,' he says, holding out his hand.

'Hughie!' my mother's yelling. 'Get her out of here now!'

The few old bids with the strength and curiosity to raise their heads from their pillows are loving it. Mum's making a scene. Hughie's pressing a hammy mit into the small of my back.

'Sorry Montse, I've dragged you here under false pretences. I should have asked Maria first. Maybe it would be for the best if you left . . . just for now.'

Well, I don't want to be here and she doesn't want me here, so why do I feel like digging my heels in? Because I don't like being pushed around.

'Ma, things are different now.' I appeal to her but she won't even look at me. As Hughie propels me out of the ward she calls out, 'And don't come back here with your filthy private ward talk!'

So I let him usher me out, but once we're on the other side of the swing doors, padding along the squeaky lino, I shrug Hughie's hand off.

'Don't try pushing me around, mate. You might get more than you bargained for.' The words are out of my mouth before I clock him properly. His bulk ain't blubber, it's brawn. Bastard's built like Giant Haystacks.

He laughs. 'Yeah, I've heard all about you, Montse and I'm shaking in my shoes. Get one thing clear, though. I'm not trying to take your mother away from you.'

'What the fuck are you talking about?'

'Maria told me you gave one or two of her boyfriends a hard time, that's all.'

Jesus! I can't believe my mother's been discussing our private business with this fucking great queen. How could she?

We've arrived at a bank of lifts and stand in silence waiting for one going down. Is he going to accompany me right off the premises? Nerve!

'Don't be like this Montse. Your mother's having her op in the morning. She's very worried about it.' He follows me into the overcrowded lift. I don't want to talk in front of all these people, looking like they've got horrible things on their minds: illness, death, madness. As soon as we hit the ground floor I shoot out, Hughie glued to my side.

'What's wrong with her anyway?'

'She's having her plumbing done.'

'Say what you mean! Having her plumbing done! What's that?'

'She's having a hysterectomy,' he says. 'And I think you should come back in the morning. See her before she goes in for the op. God forbid anything should go wrong, but if it did, you'd regret it for the rest of your life.'

'Who the hell d'you think you are? The mother–daughter police?'

'Don't be like that, Montse. Come and see her in the morning when she's calmer. They'll give her something. Make sure she gets a good night's sleep. The op's due for 10 o'clock. It's up to you. All I can do is give you the information. I'm certainly not going to beg.'

Hughie doesn't understand a thing. He hasn't given me the only piece of information I need right now. It's impossible that my mother could be in the slightest danger of dying. She's not the dying type. But I need it confirmed. Hughie hasn't said one way or the other, the thick bastard!

Roger's a very big man. So he thinks. Head honcho of Tenants Relations Officers. In his book this is big time. Prat keeps saying 'Not bad for a Barnardo's boy,' rubbing his hands together in a really irritating way. Even though he's been in the same job for three years, he still can't believe he's made it so far up the ladder of success. So insecure he never takes a holiday. When I breeze in, he's standing by my desk.

'Where've you been, Letkin? I've been paging you all morning.'

Bastard's caught me on the hop. 'Huh? Had to catch up

on my sleep, boss. Even snitches need sleep. Matter of fact, we're like vampires. Only come out in daytime in an emergency.'

'This is an emergency. Gwendoline's been asking for you.'

Could my number have come up? Have the powers that be established a connection between me and my mother? All Roger's features are squashed into the middle of his face so when he glowers he looks quite comical. Oh, it's a wind up! Why would Gwendoline want to see me?

'Oh, yeah. Sure. I believe you, Roger. How come Gwendoline wants to see me when she doesn't even remember my name?'

'That's where you're wrong, Letkin. Gwendoline knows everybody's name – and where they live.'

Maybe she wants to see me about the cock-up at Widdecombe Hall? It's just possible she might want to see me about that. Roger doesn't play jolly jokes or japes. But in the unlikely event that he's broken the habit of a lifetime, I'm not going to let him see my disbelief wavering.

'OK boss, so why does she want to see me?'

'Don't call me *boss*. We've abolished hierarchies in this town hall.'

Roger's a hoverer. He hovers by my desk while I read the message blinking on my screen: *Ring me as soon as you get in on urgent matter. Signed Karen Thompson, PA to Gwendoline Rhodes.* And he's still hovering. I look round the office to see who's tittering, pretending to be absorbed in their work while, all the time, laughing behind their monitors at the great joke they've played on Montse Letkin, office smart arse. But no one's giving themselves away. I glare at Roger till he moves.

Before calling Karen Thompson PA I get myself a coffee and try to think of all possible reasons why Gwendoline would want to see me. But the Widdecombe Hall cock-up is the only possibility I can come up with, unless I've fucked up something else without realising.

Then I'm forced to consider the very thing I hate to think about. Besides being haunted by the fear of my bosses finding out how economical I've been with the truth, creating an attractive CV for myself containing a variety of small omissions and flights of fancy. And, of course, if you've ever been a squatter or didn't pay poll tax, you ain't got a snowball's of getting a council job. Besides all that, there's more.

Among my mother's proudest souvenirs is a collection of yellowing newspaper clippings which my bosses would find interesting reading. Especially Gwendoline. In a roundabout way Gwendoline got to be Director of Housing because of my mother.

In the early 90s, Mum had her own small share of limelight. Only in the local rag of course. Nothing so grand as Gwendoline's exploits. Mum exposed a keys-for-cash scandal. Strange goings on at the estate where we were squatting. Whenever a tenant vacated, notices immediately appeared on doors naming a PIO, Protected Intended Occupier. PIO notices are meant to deter squatters from occupying voids already allocated to a future tenant. Mum asks herself: how often is the council efficient enough to fill a void straight away? Can't keep her nose out. Is that where I get my talent for snooping? Could it be genetic?

Next thing, geezers claiming to be council workers arrive at 5 a.m. to do up empty flats. In 5 a.m. Out 7 a.m.

All the new tenants are young, single, white men.

Mum sends one of her toy boys down the council claiming to be one of the named PIOs. He's given the rent book and keys to a flat. She sends down another bloke who also gets a rent book and a set of keys to a second flat.

My mother gets over-excited by her success. Like a

ditzy little *ingénue* she runs hot-foot to Orson Bainbridge, Director of Housing, with the false PIOs and rent books. Mum had a passing acquaintance with the guy from her early years in the anti-Vietnam war movement. I have a photograph of a march in which she is pushing what appears to be a pushchair laden with placards and banners. If you look carefully you can see a small foot sticking out from under the placards. Mine. Many of her old buddies from back then have now got fancy jobs in local government, drive expensive cars and live in bourgeois bliss. That's what makes me so mad! Why didn't *she* play the game? Even a normal job with a medium-sized mortgage could have meant life might have turned out different for me.

Bainbridge (known to locals as Tunbridge Wells or simply Tunbridge) takes her out to lunch and assures her he'll investigate the whole affair. Mum comes home impressed, saying Orson's got charisma.

A few days later when she's chilling down the pub with her boyfriend three heavies appear out of the woodwork offering them £800 each and a council flat for life – if they return the keys and rent books and zip their lips.

Genetically speaking, this is where me and my mother part company. Instead of accepting their generous offer, she goes blabbing to the local paper. Three o'clock in the morning the same three guys who approached them in the pub smash their way into our flat.

Sleeping peacefully in the cupboard-like box that was my bedroom I'm woken by the sound of thudding, crunching, bellowing and screaming. While I cower under my pillow, scared shitless, the heavies set upon Mum and her bloke, attacking them with baseball bats. The boyfriend retaliates with a handy crowbar. Neighbours dial triple nine. The five-o don't want to know. No statements taken. Mum ends up with broken ribs and a cauliflower nose.

Soon as she's out of hospital she again beats a path to Orson's door. He refuses to see her. Her persistent attempts to track him down lead to accusations of stalking. Was there an element of fatal attraction involved? But Maria's indignant at this interpretation. 'Fancies himself,' she says. 'Thinks he's God's gift.' Finally, she gets to confront him at a public meeting. Flustered, Bainbridge promises to get back to her in a couple of days. Next we hear he's flown the coop. Quietly copped it and hopped it. Melted into the air with severance pay. Word on the street was that he'd left the country. Somewhere down the line a vacancy was created into which stepped Gwendoline Rhodes.

After that episode — Mum hates to be reminded of it now — she goes spilling her guts to a Lib-Dem, Councillor Nesbitt, who duly contacts the police and media. This time they take notice. Crowbar man gets traded in for the councillor.

Her love life to date has been a catalogue of serial disasters involving some of the most repulsive men who ever crept the face of the earth. Take Councillor Nesbitt — please, somebody, take him! — the above-mentioned weasily little cove.

For the few months Mum was involved with him I was experiencing a rocky puberty. We go motoring in Spain *trois*-in-a-car. I was doing my first-year Spanish O-level — another examination which I never got round to taking, but which is duly entered on my CV. The councillor acted as if he and Mum were doing me a big favour, dragging me along with them to Barcelona. He got shirty when I couldn't interpret Catalonian menus. For no reason whatsoever, throughout the entire duration of the trip, the councillor insisted on referring to me as 'that stuffing, man-hating little bitch'. Mum kept schtum. P'raps I never forgave her.

Nesbitt was locked up for handing out dodgy contracts

to his mates. Yes, you could go to prison for it back then. His colleagues on the council, known as Nesbitt's Nodders, kept their heads down and lived to cheat another day.

While Ave Maria has never been keen to advertise the fact that her offspring works as an investigator for the council, neither does she wish to be reminded that she once had a dalliance with dear Councillor Nesbitt. The councillor has been airbrushed out of history.

On the positive side, if I'm getting the boot, it isn't likely to happen this way. Usually, a letter's delivered at home, by courier, early in the morning or late in the evening.

Jesus, how will I live if I get the push from this job? One thing, my Mum might start speaking to me again. That might be an improvement. But would it compensate for not being able to pay the mortgage? One geezer I know who got the push struck it lucky. Cashiers never got it together to remove his name from the payroll and his monthly salary still gets paid into his bank account. No one dobs him in. All of us hope to find ourselves in the same fortunate position some day. With my track record, I might not get that lucky. It'd be back to the bad old life for me. Hustling every penny. Living in a shithole.

Whenever I dial, the line's busy. Then, wouldn't you know, when Gwendoline's PA finally answers my gob's ramjam with flapjack.

'Come along at 5 p.m.,' she tells me. Most days I'm not in the office and when I am you don't see me hanging round the building until five, but now I'm so jittery, imagining the worst, I don't argue.

Gwendoline's office is right at the top with spectacular views of the city skyline. As the song goes, you could see Hackney Marshes if it wasn't for the houses in between. If you like that sort of thing, which I don't.

Karen's putting on her coat, preparing to leave. 'Go through. She's expecting you,' she says coldly.

Seen at close quarters Gwendoline's set-up's a revelation: at last, a definite goal to aim for! The lovely airy space, the tasteful colour scheme, the pale, silky carpet and above all, the sensation of being in the presence of a powerful woman: only the second time I've been so close. In the usual course of events, our paths would never cross. But I'll bet even my mother couldn't help being impressed if she could see me now, sitting opposite the mighty Gwendoline Rhodes, the two of us alone in her office.

'Montse, I've asked to see you because you've made a useful contribution to your department in your time here. You've certainly justified the belief I had in you. You are discreet and very effective. The fact is, Montse, I have a special task which calls for the utmost confidentiality. I've decided to entrust you with it.'

I'm keeping schtum. I didn't come down the river on a bicycle. If I had a fiver for every time I've heard shit dished up as good news I'd be stinking rich.

'I don't want to take you away from your duties for too long,' Gwendoline says. 'Only a week or so for now. I'm afraid this will mean getting in to work slightly earlier than you've been accustomed to.'

I knew it, bad news!

'Do you think you could manage that?'

'Sometimes I have to work nights.'

'I'm aware of that. Naturally, we would work around that.'

'What exactly is involved?'

'Eventually, you'll be moving up the ladder. Your unit has been targeted for a pilot project. To do with cross-border tendering. Of course, cross-border is also meant in the sense that we are now able to tender to government departments and agencies, not only to other boroughs. For example, the Widdecombe Hall operation would be of great interest to the Home Office.'

'But we already liaise with them.'

'I'm going to pretend I didn't hear that. Officially, there's no liaison at all. However, things will be a lot better when everything's put on a formal footing. Mistakes of the past can be avoided, for example, if the immigration department is supplied with more reliable information. This will involve you, Montse. You can be a part of these exciting new changes.'

Sounds like I'm headed for better things. But it always makes me laugh when the activities of my unit are presented as 100 per cent purely motivated. Council employees out there on the streets like caped crusaders, fighting racial harassment. Removing anti-social squatters. Silencing noisy neighbours. Hiring out our services to the immigration department might not fit in with this squeaky clean image. Even Gwendoline will have her work cut out to put a spin on that. Already I can see how her mind's working. Mistakes of the past can be avoided. Better information equals fewer mistakes. Fewer stiffs to account for.

'Another of the benefits of cross-border tendering is that we won't have this awful competition between ourselves and the benefit agencies to claw back money saved on fraud. That's been a perennial headache. Soon we'll be able to keep any savings that result from our own efforts. And that's good news for staff in terms of incentives.

'But, as I say, that's all in the future. Roger will be your line manager for a little bit longer and there will be no immediate salary increment. This is only temporary. Until our new project is in place. I haven't decided to whom you will report in the longer term. For now, you will report directly to me on matters concerning the special work you will do for me.'

When I hear what it is, I can hardly believe my ears.

How the hell am I going to do it? For a whole week I have to get to the office by 8.45 a.m. and go over Gwendoline's suite with an anti-bugging device. What is it, in particular, Gwendoline's worried about? No matter how unassailable she appears on the surface, I guess behind the scenes the possibilities are endless. Pick from the menu: taking kick-backs, influencing the award of contracts, using insider information to sell off council property at knock-down prices, key money, theft, gerrymandering, larceny and bribery to mention but a few.

Whatever it is, she's acting mighty cool. She certainly ain't about to entrust a lowly minion such as myself with her secrets. But she has chosen me out of the pack and in doing so makes herself a tiny bit vulnerable to me. Whether she likes it or not she has brought me into the game. I'm definitely on my way up.

Now she's telling me not to discuss this with Roger or anyone else. Not even family or friends! What family? What friends?

'What'll I say if Roger asks me what I'm doing?'

Gwendoline's got that covered. 'I suggest you take a few days off. Compassionate leave. Your mother's in hospital I believe?'

'Yes.' I only just manage to get the word out. My legs are jiggling uncontrollably and my palms are pressing down on my knees struggling to keep my feet from dancing me right out the door. My greatest nightmare has come to pass. Targeted by Gwendoline! What's the scarifying cow going to come out with next?

Although me and my mother use different surnames – Letkin and De Mesquita, no visible connection – a connection has been made. I might as well be sitting here with a bullseye on my chest.

Gwendoline's playing with her laptop as she speaks. 'It's very important for someone like me to have people around them who are totally reliable. Oh, incidentally, are you a member of the Labour Party? I know it's not a condition of employment. I only ask because if you want to demonstrate commitment by joining, you'd find a lot more doors opening.'

'I did join at one time but, erm, my membership might have lapsed . . .'

'Bear it in mind. At your age I was full of sound and fury but eventually I learnt that the world changes slowly and, even then, only if people like us use our gifts to move things in the right direction. Other people might have different agendas to ours. This is why I have to ask for your help.'

Tappitty tap, tappity tap.

'Use your imagination, Montse. A matter such as this has to be handled in a very low key manner. The fewer people who know about it the better.

'At my level there's a lot of rivalry and back-biting. I'm sure I don't have to explain to you. One has to keep ahead of the game.'

Tappitty tap.

Gwendoline, of all people, is surely ahead of the game? Her adversaries may be many but they're puny compared to her and yet she believes someone's bugging her office or planning to do so. Who'd have the nerve?

'By the way, I happened to notice from our files that your mother's been trying to get back on to our housing list for a ridiculously long time, something like ten years or more.'

Gwendoline's staring at her screen. 'According to our records she made herself intentionally homeless in the late eighties. Given the circumstances I'm afraid she'd find it practically impossible to get back into the system. That's no good, is it? It would take a small miracle but miracles can happen, Montse. They can happen. We'll have to see what can be done, won't we?'

Is this a threat or a bribe? Co-operate and Maria gets

rehoused? With my mother's record it'd take a bleeding miracle!

'Oh, by the way, I told Roger that I wanted to speak to you about Widdecombe Hall. He rather assumed I have called you in here to give you a bollocking. Let's let him go on thinking that, shall we?'

Every 'but' I raise, Gwendoline has anticipated.

'But I'll have to ask Roger for the anti-bugging equipment.' Aware I'm sounding whiny, I struggle to steady my voice. 'He signs all the requisition notes.' But this, too, she has foreseen.

'On this occasion, Montse,' she says with a hint of acid, 'we won't be asking Roger for a requisition note. That would hardly be keeping the matter confidential, would it?'

I have to agree. She consults her fat gold watch. Waiting on her desk is an envelope containing the exact money, labelled with the address of a specialist electronics shop where I'm to buy the necessary gadgetry. She hands over the loot. Neatly printed on the outside of the envelope is a list of items and their cost.

Bug detector: £646.25p
Digital line guard £795
Total including VAT: £1,441.25p

'Er, sorry Ms Rhodes, but I've just thought of another problem. Won't it look a bit bad if I go straight out of here and ask Roger for compassionate leave when I've just had a so-called bollocking from you?'

A dry laugh comes from her direction though her face remains expressionless. 'Don't worry about Roger. You won't have to work with him for very much longer.'

God! The creepy way she says it, I'm almost feeling sorry for the guy.

three

MY HEART JUDDERS on entering the gynae ward. Suffocating sun streams in through the windows. Baking beds have been abandoned, patients gone for a smoke or to watch breakfast TV. Day staff mostly white.

When I spot my mother my jaw drops. Her bed's been moved right in front of the nursing station. She's sitting up on her pillows grinning. If this pleasantry is directed at me it's bloody embarrassing.

'Hullo baby. Nice day for it, innit?'

I approach the bed. 'Mum, why are you having a hysterectomy? If it's just the fibroids, why not wait a few years. Till they carbonate, or whatever.'

'Carbonate?'

I've never heard her laugh so much. Tears gush down her pebble-dash face.

'Pass me a tissue, Montse.' She blows her knobbly nose, honking loudly. When she calms down she's still smiling.

'Hughie's round somewhere,' she says. 'Gone off to get himself a coffee. He's been so good, old Hughie. A real sweetie.'

'Mum! What are you on?'

The giggling breaks out again. 'Tee hee hee. What am

I on? I dunno. But I wish I could get a ton of it to take home with me. Ask the nurse. She's a sweetie.'

'Mum, do you realise that a hysterectomy is the most-performed unnecessary operation? Are you sure you know what you're doing?'

'Leave it out, Montse. It's too late now. I've signed the thingmy. Hee hee.'

For years me and my mother haven't been able to exchange more than a few words without one or both of us going nuclear. Even now I can feel myself getting wound up with anxiety and anger. Her manic grin. Calling people sweeties! It ain't normal.

'Back in a jiff, Mum.'

The nurse informs me it's the pre-med they've dispensed, Omnipon, that's caused her relentless camaraderie. Better make the most of it while I can.

'Hey, Mum. You know what you said about my job? Well, things have changed.'

Mum's going in and out, eyes rolling. I have to speak quite loudly. 'I'm working direct for Gwendoline Rhodes now. Me are Gwendoline are like this.' I hold up two fingers pressed together. Her eyes are open and this sets her off again, giggling. 'Listen Mum, a lot of what I do really helps people.'

But the old orbs are rolling again. 'Mum, listen! Sometimes people need a witness. No one will come forward. Especially when it's racial harassment. I am that witness! I'm always in court. Giving evidence that helps people get rehoused. Mum?'

'Excuse me.' A nurse appears brandishing a syringe on a dish. 'We need to give your mother a little injection to make her nice and drowsy. Would you mind waiting outside? I'm going to pull the curtain.'

How drowsy can you get? Mum's already well out of it.

But she opens one eye and mumbles, 'Don't mind her, nurse. She's seen my bum often enough.'

But I can't remember seeing her backside or any other part of her. Not naked. Then she rolls over, obligingly lifting the back of her nightie, and the nurse plunges the needle deep into her mottled rump. All my blood rushes from my head down to my feet. When I try to move, I can't. My feet are too full of blood.

In seconds Mum's conked out in a gormless slumber. The nurse whips a hairnet over her lolling head and rolls a pair of tight surgical stockings right up to her thighs.

'Stops clots forming,' she explains.

I gag into my hand. 'Thank you for sharing.'

Just before ten, Hughie appears. Bending over the bed he takes one of Mum's liver-spotted hands in his big doughy ones.

'Maria, can you hear me? I'll be right here when you wake up. Don't worry about anything. You're going to be fine.' His cheeks are wet. Who does he think he is anyway? None of his fucking business!

Some guys come along with a gurney and it's 'one-two-three-hup'. They load her like a sack of spuds. Just before they wheel her off I jump forward and give her a peck on the chin. Hughie looks so smug I wish I hadn't done it.

'What're you looking at?'

'You, Montse. You.'

I hate this creepy feeling that Mum and Hughie are the adults and I'm relegated to being a child. Plomping myself down in the visitors' chair, I feel paper rustling. Dragging a newspaper out from under me, I hold it up in front of my face like a shield.

'What're you going to do now?' Hughie asks.

'Gotta get to work, of course.' Of course nothing. As from this morning I'm on compassionate leave but how can I tell that to Hughie? 'Don't you geddit, you great fucking queen? It's only because of the drugs she's even speaking to me!'

Hughie doesn't answer. Once more I concentrate on the paper with its baffling headline: *Old Left to Die*. Didn't that go toes up aeons ago?

Leaving my wheels in the hospital car park I set off, legging it through the gridlocked traffic towards Baker Street, trying not to think of Mum and the surgeon's knife.

Shop's aglow with squirly neon. Heavy glass door won't give way even when I lean my whole body weight against it. Won't budge. Now I notice a buzzer, press it and fall in the door. Trembly old lech with mutton chop sideburns leers from behind a showcase, delighted at my discomfiture. My story is I'm representing my boss, a big wheel in a privatised utility (not such a lie) who thinks a rival is out to get her.

'Don't be embarrassed,' he says. 'We've heard it all before. You don't have to explain. You've got nothing to be ashamed of. Most of the equipment we sell is for defensive purposes. I'd say 99 per cent. No need for embarrassment.'

He shows me a range of interesting debuggers. I don't tell him that I already know the exact piece of equipment I have to buy. His sales patter's too fascinating. Eventually I pick out the pieces which Gwendoline had pre-selected. I notice a pile of catalogues lying on the counter – they're twenty quid each! So if you add that to the £1,441.25p, she ain't getting much change out of a grand-and-a-half.

Me plates give out on the way back through the park so I find a quiet place to sit by the canal, debugger beside me on the bench. We came here to feed the ducks when I was a nipper. I kick off my trainers and massage my aching soles. Strange that I should have returned to this spot while Mum's having our physical connection – the pouch I emerged from – surgically removed.

Barefoot in the park I take a letter from my pocket. A letter in my mother's large, square handwriting full of underlinings and exclamations, every word engraved on my brain. After our bust-up over my job, she wrote to me in the style of her Maoist phase. Since then I have come to understand the letter was a form of closure, her old leftie obsession with setting out the history of a phenomenon, as she sees it, and sending copies to all concerned. Except in our case we were the only two concerned. And even she is not all that concerned.

The letter's grey with wear, the paper only hanging together by a few fibres. First I rip along the fold lines. Then I tear each piece in half and keep doing it till I have a fistfull of confetti.

'*Montserrat, my only daughter* (note that, no dear, dearest or darling for moi!),

'*Look upon this as my last testament. Do not destroy this. Read on. Do not react in your customary manner by tearing this up in a rage before digesting my words. It causes me great pain to write this and I understand you will find it difficult to grasp why I am so hard on you.*'

Difficult to grasp. A difficult concept to grasp. The comrades used that word a lot. Grasp.

'*When you informed me with such glee that you are now employed as a paid informer for Gwendoline Rhodes, I could scarely believe my ears – I mean this literally, my tinnitus has got worse. Now I have taken it in I can safely say this is the lowest point in my life. Gwendoline Rhodes and her ilk have plans to force working people to live in "appropriate accommodation". People in two-bedroomed flats will be forced into one-bedroomed places. People in one-bedroomed places will be forced into bed-sits. People in bed-sits will be forced into hostels and if you are in a hostel you will go onto the streets.*

'As I understand it, you are the Judas who gives the council the names of the candidates for living-space (Lebensraum) demotion; and who knows what other horrors you are called upon to precipitate and facilitate. What I cannot understand is your motive. Is it as was observed after the rise of the Nazis? Each time society, through unemployment, frustrates the small person in his or her normal functioning and normal self-respect, it trains them for that last stage in which they will willingly undertake any function, even that of hangman.

'Out of my womb' – Her womb, that treacherous organ! – *'Out of my womb I have begotten a duplicitous class traitor who has not only given comfort to the same enemy whom I have fought tooth and nail for my entire life, but has joined them, wholeheartedly, unashamedly and completely. Where is your loyalty? Where is your imagination? What was in your mind when you announced the news so proudly, "Mum, I've got a job", like some petit bourgeois little school leaver?*

'Youth is no excuse. Younger than you are now, I devoted myself to the struggle for social justice, people's liberation and true democracy. Such words mean nothing to you although you have heard them from my lips many times.

'I had high hopes of you. Your intelligence and courage as a child led me to believe that you would join the struggle, that you would add your grain of sand, as we all must, in the process of changing the world.'

When my nursery teacher told me Guy Fawkes was a villain, I was at first perplexed, then angry. This was not what my mother had taught me. I was furious. My illusion of the teacher's infallibility was shattered. How could you trust someone who got things so wrong?

'Remember "The Foolish Old Man Who Moved Mountains"? And "The Cock Crowed at Midnight"? You loved those childhood stories. In my naiveté I imagined they would act as

an antidote to ruling class, market forces, no pain no gain propaganda. But no, you are up to your eyebrows in the reactionary cesspool.

'I have heard it said that you are an exile in your own country when you cannot understand the language. I understand it, but I cannot bring myself to speak it. I have the words, but can say no more. Speaking to my own daughter is like speaking into a scrambler. I am now truly living in the interstices, an exile in my own country!'

Snot's building up in my sinuses when a shockingly familiar figure breaks into my line of vision. I almost shout, 'Hey, Mum!' Her doppelganger. Older, and with a more pronounced waddle, the resemblance is powerful enough to spook me out of the pits.

The woman passes without a glance, stopping further along the bank. I watch her open a plastic carrier bag, take out a loaf of bread and break it into bits for the ducks. Moving further away, she attempts to conceal herself behind a tree. But I lean forward and keep her in view. First she throws chunks of bread on to the water. The ducks zoom in. Slyly, she scatters a few crumbs on the concrete bank. One by one the ducks emerge from the canal. The bread drops closer and closer to the woman's feet until a bold Muscovy advances right up to her toes. The woman pounces. Her arm shoots out. She has the bird by the neck. A quick twist and the thing's in the carrier bag. Ready-stuffed bird in a bag.

Standing with my toes over the edge of the concrete bank, I observe my foreshortened reflection. Long-legged. Pin-headed. I lob the ball of shredded paper on to my watery image and it disintegrates into swirly circles. A flotilla of paper petals drifts away, disappearing under a bridge.

Tempus fugit, as Stan would say.

Mum's lying there with a big rubber gobstopper in her gob.

'Hughie! What's that in her mouth?'

'Just something to help them breathe and make sure they don't swallow their tongues.'

A nurse comes to change the porridgy bag of pee hanging off the end of Mum's catheter and we are sent to stand on the other side of the curtain.

'Do y' think she'll still be talking to me when the drugs wear off?'

'Probably.'

'We had a good chat this morning.'

'Yeah?'

'Yeah. About my job n'that. I think she understands it better now.'

Suddenly Hughie's huffing and puffing. 'Look, Montse,' he says, jabbing his forefinger at me. 'This ain't about you. It's about *her!* She's the one who's lying in a hospital bed. Not you!'

I'm not taking this from any fucker. I don't care who it is. So, thanks to that little toe rag, I walk out without seeing my Mum come round.

Facing the exit on the ground floor there's seating for patients, ex-patients and their families. People in splints, plaster casts, pregnant, not pregnant, sweet, sour, smelly, fragrant, fat, skinny, young, old, drunk, sober, you name it. Waiting for transport. Ask the receptionist and she'll call you a mini-cab. Or, maybe next week, an ambulance will turn up. The misshapen chairs are screwed to the floor. Who'd want to steal a naff plastic chair? It'd be easier to steal a baby. Rather have the chair meself.

Bang in the middle of this sea of miserable cases, there's a familiar face under a round crocheted hat. Older, thinner, more melancholy than I remember, but definitely my old school chum, Louise.

Her face brightens when she clocks me. 'Long time,' she cries, jumping up. Painted pegs for earrings, ropes of multi-coloured beads round her neck and a keffiah with a small bundle in it looped across her back. A right hippy. Our cheekbones collide.

'What're you up to, Montse?'

'Been visiting my Mum upstairs.'

'Your Mum! Wow, I remember her. Hope it's nothing serious.'

'Nah, nah, she'll be fine. You?'

'What does it look like?'

Bloody hell, it's a baby on her back!

'Where'd you geddit?'

'His name's Puja, and he was born yesterday.'

'Well, I wasn't. So whose is he?'

'Still the joker, Montse. You haven't changed.'

I offer to drive her wherever she's going and as we walk to the car, she talks. Weezie always liked to talk a lot and for once I don't mind listening.

'His dad's a shaman,' she says.

'Y' whah? I thought it took years and years to be one of them!'

'You might remember him, Montse. He was in our year at school. He was called Nigel back then but now he's called Nirvana.'

'Sounds a modest kind of guy.'

'Actually, you may scoff, but he is modest, considering his gifts.'

'Glad to hear it.'

'He would have been here for the birth, but he had to go on a vision quest.'

Automatically, I open the passenger door but she tells me she has to get in the back because of Poojar. When we were at school everyone thought of Louise as a complete airhead. Blow in her ear and she'd say, 'Thanks for the refill.' But it's clever the way she's tied the thing on her back. When she gets in the car she unwinds the bundle and out of the folds emerges this tiny screwed up face, a round crocheted hat like Weezie's pulled down over its ears. Deep worry lines on the forehead, and it's only one day old! Boy, you're right to be worried. Stick round kid. You ain't seen nothing yet.

'Where to, Weezie?'

'God, Montse, no one's called me that since school.'

'Yeah?' Looking back, I think it might have been me who gave her the stupid name in the first place.

'I'm going back to my hostel,' she says, 'down the hill, first right, then I'll direct you from there. Wow, what a fantastic car.'

'It's my Mum's.'

'She's got a car? That's amazing. She used to be so against cars. Remember when she tried to pull the bull bars off that Range Rover outside the school?'

I'm fiddling with the keys. Delaying.

'Hey, what are you doing in a hostel?'

'Where do you think homeless women go when they're pregnant? I can't go to my mum. My sister and her two kids are there already.'

'What's this hostel called?'

'Widdecombe. Know it?'

'Nope.' All I can think is that some time in the next forty-eight hours Widdecombe Hall is going to be raided. It will be in the early hours of the morning when the overstayers and other illegals are tucked up for the night, dreaming of happy families. The guys who do the raids are not bad people, I know some of them. Just doing their jobs, same as I do mine, not getting any particular pleasure out of it. Just earning a living.

Knowing that, there's no way I'm taking Weezie and Poojar back there.

'What's up, Montse?'

'Just thinking. What's this hostel like then?'

'Nice. Warm. I've met some lovely women there. The place isn't too clean, though. Roaches.'

I twist in my seat. 'Tell you what, why don't we go to my Mum's flat? It'd be much nicer for the baby. I've got her keys. Looking after the place while she's in the hossie. It's got central heating and there's no roaches. How about it?'

Weezie's hesitant. How can she prefer a roach-infested shithole to a nice, comfortable flat?

'It's just that I've made some good friends in the hostel. They'll be waiting for me. Dying to know whether I've had a boy or a girl and how the birth went 'n that. And I've got to go back there some time, so I might as well go now. Really kind of you to think of it though.'

A moving wall of metal streams past us, bumper to bumper. Bastards. I'm never going to get out of here. My nose is moving out inch by inch.

'Watch it, Montse!' Weezie cries.

My foot flies off the clutch and we shoot into the stream of cars, the geezer behind us blowing his horn in a nutzoid fashion.

'What's his fucking problem?'

'Well, you did cut him up,' Weezie says. 'And, I'm sorry Montse, but we're going completely the wrong way. It's down the hill and first right.'

'Fuck Widdecombe Hall. We're going to Mum's flat. Ring your mates from there.'

Weezie exclaims over the delightfulness of my abode.

'Wow. I can't believe your mother's got this place. She must have really opened herself up to prosperity.'

'Yeah. She did.'

'It's a bit sterile, though. Everything seems to be brand new.'

'Yeah. A bit unlived in. Mum hasn't been here long.'

'What does she do? I mean, you know, for a living?'

I've been so busy diverting Weezie's attention from Widdecombe Hall and her waiting mates that I haven't thought up a good answer to this question.

'Um, to be honest, we haven't been in touch for a while. It's only since she got ill I've been involved with her again. We've got a lot of catching up to do. Like you and me. Hey, you know what! It's dinner time. Are you feeling peckish? I've got some barley wine. Let's wet the baby's head. And I've got the kind of food you like. Remember those fry-ups we used to have at midnight?'

'Have you got any brown rice?'

Weezie's inspecting the kitchen, making me nervous. 'Wow, you wouldn't think someone going into hospital would stock up so much food,' she says, opening and closing cupboard doors.

Why didn't I tell her I had a job? Some other job? Off the cuff I can't think of any job acceptable to someone like Weezie. You don't earn the kind of money it takes to buy a pad like this unless you're prepared to compromise yourself. I don't come clean because I want her to stay a while. And that's just the way it is.

We eat scrambled egg on toast with our plates balanced on our laps. She refuses ketchup. Poojar's playing dead. I have to keep touching his fingers and watching his breath. Weezie's worried about not having enough nappies. She's brassic.

'I have to go back to the hostel tomorrow,' she says, 'to pick up my giro.'

I dig fifty quid from my pants pocket. She's reluctant.

'Hey, take it! I won a few quid on the lottery.'

'You've been doing the lottery? Oh no, my blood boils to see so many poor people queueing up at the post office to buy lottery tickets. Sick people, people in wheelchairs.'

'Yeah, me too. The lottery's a mug's game. I only did it this one time and I felt bad.'

She only agrees to take the money when I put it to her as if she's doing me a favour. Get a bit of shopping, toilet rolls and stuff.

'Tomorrow, I'll make lunch,' she says firmly. 'Then I'll go back to Widdecombe tomorrow evening if that's OK with you. I really need to go and pick up my giro.'

After that's settled we get down to catching up on each other's current lives. But the present's too dodgy. I have to keep diverting the conversation back to the past. It's safer.

'Remember the school trip to Dachau?'

That gets her going. 'Those teachers must have been crazy. Taking a group of totally unaware teenagers to a place like that.'

Angrily, Louise screws up her face recalling how our classmates had scribbled 'kill wogs and queers' all over the pristine, white walls at the death camp memorial.

'And poor Shelley. What they did they do to her? She was screwed up for years after that trip.'

'Don't ask me.'

Shelley was the class drongo. We tattooed 'My mum's a bull dagger' on her forehead.

Suddenly the clammy atmosphere charges up. Outside the sky flashes and a few seconds later a rolling thunderclap whipcracks over our heads. Weezie flings open the window. Rain's belting down, hammering on the roofs and tinkling into drains. She leans out to enjoy the downpour. 'Oh, it's so beautiful. Doesn't the rain sound exactly like gamelan?'

'Huh! Probably acid rain.'

In the small hours, when the storm's passed, I dress stealthily, creeping out of my luxurious flat like a criminal. Only the moon knows I'm out and about. Swollen and yellow like a big ugli fruit in the sky, she oversees every move I make as I drive towards Widdecombe.

Lights are blazing, the front door's hanging wide open. There's a paddy wagon in the driveway, beacon flashing. The pigeons have been shut out, their access hole blocked off with a bit of chipboard. They're tearing at the barrier with their beaks.

Immigration boys swarming all over the gaff. Couple of guys drag someone out. Silhouettes in the doorway. Arms strapped to sides. Taped mouth, sagging knees. They lob him in the back of the van and lean against the doors, having a fag and chatting. Waiting for someone. A woman screams at them from a window above but they're acting like nothing's happening. Discussing football.

Provoking stares I sidle over and start to mount the steps.

'Just a minute, miss. You can't go in there.'

Now I really can hear the commotion. Voices raised. Heavy footsteps. Doors slamming. I show the two goons my ID. Still suspicious, they let me pass.

Sally's darting about in the hall.

'Montse! What are you doing here?'

'Old mate of mine, wears long skirts, hair scraped back. Through no fault of her own, yeah? Landed up here.'

'Right. Know who you mean. That'd be Louise, wouldn't it? Her room's on the second floor. You should have said, Montse. I didn't know she was a mate of yours.'

Upstairs, I find Trevor, a guy I met a few times at clubs, who's searching Weezie's room. Doesn't even look surprised to see me.

'Bloody hippies,' he says examining Weezie's stuff, 'they think the world owes them a living.'

I could smash his sneering face as he holds up one of Poojar's tiny outfits, pulling stuff out of a bag, then throwing it on the floor and trampling on it. Poojar's only been in this fucking world a couple of days and Trevor's already walking all over his stuff.

'Hey, Trevor. Do me a favour. This is an unofficial visit. So happens a mate of mine's ended up in here. Not illegal. I went to school with her. Yeah, bit of a hippy, but she's got a little kid and, just as a favour, I said I'd collect her stuff. She's staying with me for a while.'

'Oh, Christ. You should've said, Montse. Why didn't you say? I didn't realise. Gotta look after our kith 'n kin, don't we?' Winks. Me and Trevor? Got something in common?

'Yeah, that's it, Trev. We gotta look after our own.'

Trevor's assumption that him and me are kith 'n kin blows my mind. Is there a grain of truth in it? Is that how others see me?

'Can I borrow one of these?' He's got black bin-liners marked 'Immigration Service'. I'm stuffing Weezie and Poojar's things into the plastic sacks without waiting for his answer. Apparently, he's vexed. 'Er. OK.' he says rattily. 'I'll be next door.'

Boot leather hits timber. More crying and shouting. I'm shoving everything moveable into bags. Packages of nappies. Clothes. Music tapes. Candles. Incense burner. All the new agey trappings you'd expect. Plus picture albums. School photos. Flinging the bulging bags over my shoulders, I pound down the stairs.

'Hey you!'

'It's OK! Trevor said.'

'But. Fucking hell . . .' They gape at each other but they don't stop me. I shove the lot in the back of my motor and streak off like a bat out of hell.

Carrying a briefcase containing the Spymaster equipment, I ascend to Gwendoline's Eyrie in the skyrie.

'Dress for it,' Gwendoline had ordered. First time I've dressed smart to ride in an elevator. All because, rather than risk people seeing me going in the front, she's got me a swipe card to use the special entrance round the back.

As I arrive on the top floor I see Stan, ahead of me in the corridor, also on the job early. Wearing stiff denim overalls. Carrying his tool bag. Whistling jauntily. He goes to the door of the women's loo next to Gwendoline's office and puts up a 'closed for repair' sign.

When Stan was made foreman he started wearing civvies. Plumbing jobs no longer his usual concern. The overall looks odd on him now. Him and I aren't best mates since I had a skinful and sang 'The working class can kiss my arse, I've got the foreman's job at last' down the pub. Man can't take a joke!

Right now Mr Motormouth's the last person I want to see.

Going on tip-toe, silently opening Gwendoline's office with the pass key, quietly closing the door after me: I find I needn't have bothered. A brass band wouldn't be heard over the din in this place. Couple of cleaners are shouting gossip over the vacuuming. Radio blaring. They go bug-eyed when I walk in in my glad rags.

'Sorry Ms Rhodes, we're just finishing up.'

So, it's true. Clothes maketh the woman!

'Get a move on then. Go on, hop it.' Out go the cheeky

bitches, making faces. Man, if I really was Gwendoline they'd be collecting their cards toot sweet.

Following the simple procedure I was shown in the shop, I install the £795.04p digital line guard. From now on Gwendoline can have complete peace of mind phone-wise.

What I love most about my job, apart from the fact that it's not shit pay and it's not shit work, is the gadgets. Take this cute little debugger for instance, all tucked up in its carry-case snug as a bug. Attach it to a telescopic stick and it reaches the ceiling. Over she goes, down the walls, across the carpet, behind the desk. Not a sausage. Waste of time. That Gwendoline's such a paranoid cow!

On a hostess trolley contraption near her desk there's an espresso machine and a baggie of coffee. So I brew up a cup and have a snoop around. Dragon Lady isn't due for another half hour.

Laid out on an architect's drawing board, the kind you have to mount a high stool to reach, is a laminated map of London, the boroughs marked out in red lines like a battle ground. Pinned to one side, the Prime Minister's fax number is casually scrawled on a memo pad! To me, this is an important revelation which denotes something which I'm surprised I had not thought of before, given Gwendoline's well-known ambition: the map convinces me that Gwendoline Rhodes fancies herself as Mayor of London!

The balcony invites. I get the door open and step out. Petrified by heights, I'm madly attracted by my own vertigo. Out here there's an ugly concrete wall which I can't see over unless I stand on tiptoe. I reckon I'm the same height as Gwendoline. Does she ever come out here? A few aluminium chairs and a folding table have been arranged as if for a drinks party. I see her on a summer's day with a bottle of chilled wine, wheeling and dealing down her mobile.

When I insert my toes into an aperture a few inches

from the ground and stretch my arms out full-length, my fingertips just reach the edge of the wide concrete parapet which separates me from empty space. An eerie otherworldly thrumming drifts up from the traffic crawling in the streets below. My eyes have gone migrainy and when I suddenly imagine: what if I was hanging on the other side of the parapet, my feet dangling into space? I freak myself out so bad that I emit a silly little scream, scraping my knuckles and drawing blood as I flop onto the balcony.

four

ONCE A MONTH THERE'S a knees-up at the Red Carnation Club. Fund-raisers for the local party. Raising peanuts. Big smells get to glad-hand the rank and file. Social mixing of the third kind. Plenty of suckers to lap it up. Hi-ya here, back-clap there. Couple of drinks and they're anybody's. And our great leaders are up and out the door like rats up a sewer. Back to their real lives, leaving us with the cheap beer, candles in bottles, and red light bulbs. It's that kind of place. Peer into the gloomy corners and you can make out the underfives play equipment and stinky yoga mats, stacked out of sight of sophisticated clubbers.

My attendance is not expected. Officially I'm on compassionate leave. Karen's looking at me funny. Karen's a regular. In the absence of her boss, she's Gwendoline's surrogate, allowing herself to be shmoozed like there's no tomorrow. Later tonight Gwendole's scheduled to put in one of her rare appearances, to present a cheque to a playgroup partly funded by the council. Couple of small businesses looking for a reduction in local property taxes are going to make a donation. Big deal.

Nine o'clock. No Gwendoline. In my fantasy I disregard the fact that she's forbidden me to approach her in public. Au contraire, she greets me as an old and trusted colleague, invites me to her table, packed with glitterati. From now on we are firm friends.

Stanley's holding forth at the bar, hair slickered old-rocker style. Let's be nice. Make up for previous misdemeanours.

'Ah, Miss Nutkin, what's your tipple?' Thinks he's the dog's bollocks wearing a vision-impairing mustard jacket and dicky bow. Where's the clothes police when y' need 'em? My tipple? One part Southern Comfort, one part vodka over ice, in a tall glass topped up with dry ginger. Stan winces as he opens his wallet.

'You're looking gorgeous tonight, Stan. I prefer you in a boiler suit, though.'

'I haven't worn one of those for years.' He seems annoyed.

'I know that, Stan, I only meant I prefer the proletarian look.'

'If it's my body you're after, Mizz Nutkin, I'm already spoken for. I'm a family man. Right, Vinnie?'

'Right!' Vinnie, from the borough treasurer's office, buries his long pointed nose in his pint and sniggers.

'Thought Gwendoline'd be here tonight.'

'Nah. She wouldn' come here,' Vinnie sneers.

'Wasn't she gonna present a cheque to a kids' project?'

'Maybe, but I heard she's got problems.'

'Who? Gwendoline?'

'Yeah. I know the bloke who's shagging her secretary.'

'What! He must be some pathetic bastard.'

'Nope. Ambitious bastard. 'Cording to Karen, the Dragon Lady's been acting really whacko.' Vinnie's leaning towards me talking out the side of his mouth like a gangster. 'Seeing a therapist in her lunch hour. One of those yank-style shrink-mobiles. Drives round for an hour getting her head read.'

I find Vinnie's story incredible. Shrinks are so-called

because they make you feel small. You have to be in awe of your shrink. From what I've seen of her Gwendoline Rhodes is in awe of nobody.

Vinnie's looking over his shoulder. 'Uh oh. Watch out. Here comes the oil slick.'

Roger's hovering. Stan condescends a quick nod in his direction, dismissing him. At work, Roger's a commissar but outside the town hall, up at the bar, it's Stan the Man who's top dog. Stan has established himself in double quick time. Union man, darts player, pool player, betting *aficionado*, always has good craic, always gives the impression he knows more than he's letting on. I could learn from Stan.

If you're not accepted by his group, or on parlaying terms, you're on the at-risk register socially. Roger knows this but he doesn't know how to go about rectifying it. All he can do is hover. Not fitting in here, with the grass roots, and not fitting in there, with the bureaucrats, where he belongs. My nightmare. To be like Roger.

No one invites me, I always have to push myself forward. It's a piss off: the bigger my pay cheque the fewer friends I have. Innit s'pose to work the other way? So I stand here drinking with Stan the Man. By now he's collected a large group. Vinnie dishing the dirt about expense account splurges, Lou from estate management, going on about how many times he's had sex in a void, – 'Hey, Lou,' Vinnie screams. 'Have you ever had it any other way?' Ha ha. And Millie, who used to be Karen's assistant but demanded a transfer because she couldn't hack it.

'She cuss me down in front of a lift full of councillors. She shout through the toilet door while I'm changing me pussy claht. That Gwendoline woman never took my complaint seriously.'

Stan shakes his head and draws his bushy eyebrows together in solidarity, 'I'm not against women getting on.

Don't get me wrong. But things have gone too far the other way.' He pauses and rolls his eyes as Millie walks off in disgust. 'You've got these women like Gwendoline Rhodes modelling themselves on Thatcher. They're taking over the world! You won't believe this but I remember when she was called Red Gwen.'

Vinnie gets in a round while Stan recites the same old Gwendoline stories. Then Vinnie starts,

'Hey, Montse. I ever tell you about the time I caught the great she-elephant with suitcases full of folding money?'

'No, Vinnie. I don't believe I've heard that one.'

One particular year, so long ago that Vinnie's sure there's no harm telling me — it'll make me laugh — the council was allowed to sell off its assets. But there was a rule that any deals had to be completed by 31st December. They sell a building right on the deadline. Vinnie claims he sees the Finance Director at the New Year's rave. Vinnie has to clamber over the Bolly bottles. Gwendoline and the finance geezer have got two million quid in notes piled up on the floor. They were trying to count it, but they were too pissed.

'Don't lie!'

He buys me another drink.

'It's fucking true, Montse. You better believe it. They were too pissed to count it and I had to count it. Took me hours to get it all bagged up and stowed in the safe. What d'you reckon to that?'

'Nobody trousered none?'

'Not that I saw. But the odd few hundred quid wouldn't have been missed.'

My guess is this happened to someone else who told it to Vinnie and he's appropriated the story and put himself in it. Time to attach myself to another group.

'Gotta take the load off me plates,' I tell Vinnie and saunter off. There's a space at a table nearby.

Now I'm sitting I feel as if I'm in a boat and I can't tell whether it's the boat or the shore that's moving. Suddenly the shore seems a long way off. I've pushed the boat out. Little geezer next to me who I've never seen before, starts chatting. Narrow shoulders, dug-out chest, telling me how he's come down from somewhere in the stix and wants to stay in the city. Man'd last two minutes. Telling me how he's standing in front of this posh restaurant reading the menu when a bouncer comes out and goes 'fuck off out of here or I'll call the police'.

'All I was doing was looking at the menu, right?'

No interior monologue going on. No thinking in sentences. He's the kind of guy who's so cut off from his surroundings he'd carrying on yakking about his personal shit even if he was on a scenic trip through the Grand Canyon. All this I am able to deduce in a couple of minutes. Gawd, now he's rabbitting about his mother.

'... didn't get in till one in the morning. There she is, sitting at the table in her coat. Well vexed. Shouting the odds.'

He goes trembly at the memory. 'Like "you've got to go to college," right? None of her business. She didn't bring me up, right? My gran brought me up. I always thought of my gran as my mother. She brought me up, not her!'

His racoon eyes fill with tears. Now I get it. Verbal diarrhoea's his way of jumping up and down yelling 'I'm here. I exist!' Poor little tosser.

'Hey, I'm Montse.' I shake his hand like a big sister. 'My mother's a bit of a dipstick too.'

'Were you adopted?'

'Nah, if only! A dysfunctional mother is worse. I keep thinking my real mother's going to come and claim me. But unfortunately, just my luck, the woman I know as my mother *is* my real mother.'

I'm playing for laughs, but he doesn't laugh. 'Aren't you

a bit old to be waiting for your mother to claim you?' he says bitchily, distracted from his own tale of woe for a nanosecond. Before he can start monologuing again, I jump in,

'So what's your name?'

'Billy.'

'Hi Billy. What are you doing here tonight? Are you in the local party?'

'What fucking party?' No, of course not, he lives out of town. He's come here to wait for his mother to show up so he can hit on her for money. Here's my chance to get back at him for his nasty reaction to my little joke about my Mum. But, no. I'm in an expansive mood now, a woman with few friends who collects waifs and strays. We exchange telephone numbers, then as in a dream, when a human being turns into an animal or another person, or just disappears, my new friend vanishes into the ether. Right now if anyone asked me to repeat the conversation we just had, I wouldn't be able to.

'Yo, Montse. Nuff respect!' Trolling towards me is Tony, a clerk from the Borough Solicitor's office. Man's got an identity problem. Thinks he's black.

'How's Sarah?' I ask him having got over my wobbly. As soon as I have another drink I get a second wind.

Tony's missus is one of those local government femocrats Stan complains about, crashing through the glass ceiling like a bunch of lemmings. Power-dressed to kill. Sarah got a new big job reorganising parking in the borough. Made a name for herself streamlining her last department by applying liposuction. I'd like to have a go at her about the parking arrangements outside Widdecombe Hall.

One time when Tone and me were drinking together he confided in me how he fucks his wife while she's asleep. And I quite liked the geezer till he told me that.

'Sarah couldn't make it tonight, babe. Gotta report to

write. Crucial nuff important stuff for the P & R committee. Hey, guess who's here tonight?'

'Who?'

Tone's accent suddenly relocates from Hackney to Highgrove. 'Orson Bainbridge,' he whispers in awe. 'Chap got a massive severance pay-off a few years ago. Been living in South America for yonks. Now he's working for a big City consultant. PKMG, one of those.'

So, Tunbridge is back in town. What will Maria make of that? I was just a little kid. Can't even remember what he looked like, this man who changed my mother's face and was always a big presence in our lives after that. Or is his importance only in my head? Not entirely. My mother talked about him nearly every day since. P'raps he doesn't even know what he did to us and the deep way his actions affected the two of us.

Tone says Orson's angling for a long-term contract. Financial consultant to the council.

Tone's swivelling eye sockets make me feel queasy as he desperately searches for a gap where he can insert himself at a suitable table. Before he can bolt, I engage him with questions,

'Is Sikowits doing the floorshow tonight? I thought he was finished long time ago.'

'Guy's had a rough time. He's on the comeback trail though. Tonight Red Carnation. Tomorrow Madam Jo Jo's!'

'Oh yeah? Hey, by the way, Tone, can you tell me which one's Orson Bainbridge? I heard he's a guy who's got charisma.'

'Front of the bandstand. On his own.'

Thick blond-white hair. Horn-rim bifocals. Tasteful silk jacket.

'Let's go over.'

'We can't.'

'Why not? It's a free country.' I drag Tony by the arm. The crowd are calling for Sikowits. Nobody's shown up with a cheque for the nursery. As we pass I'm earwigging on Karen's table. A woman from a childcare campaign is trying to make herself heard above the braying of Gwendoline's frustrated sycophants. Making do with the monkey while longing for the organ-grinder to appear none of them are listening to each other, raving on about best value, global financial models, information flows, forward planning rationalisation. They've got their own lingo. Word games. Take away a word. Put another word. Take away labour, put human resources. Take away equality, put fairness. Take away contracting out, put externalisation. And so on. You need to know the lingo if you wanna be an upwardly mobile wannabe.

'Hi there, Mr Bainbridge. Tone, hop to it, mate. Get Mr Bainbridge a drink and I'll have the same again! What's going on, Orson! Is it just me or are the lights getting dim?'

Tony makes his getaway. Bainbridge adjusts his chair, Browns-clad back turned to me. Who does he fucking think he is? All the lights have gone out. A spotlight rakes the tables flicking over my face, probing my eyelids before moving to the stage.

An MC comes out. Snaking the lead of the mike, he introduces Sikowits in a nasal put-on voice. Usually, I like chilling with a few jars, enjoying a bit of live entertainment, but now I feel grotsville 'cause my glass is empty.

The comedian prances on. Tuxedo and tights. Rats-tail hair. Grabs the mike. Screams, 'Nigger, nigger, nigger!' There's a few titters. 'That's just to clear the air,' he rants.

Look at Tony. Tony's smiling. They're all white and they're all laughing. Except me. Suddenly I'm going crazy. The geezer on stage picks up an inflatable doll and pretends to bonk it. 'That's in case there's any feminists out there,' he bawls.

'What's pink, hard and cold?' Shrieks of laughter.

'Cot death.'

They love it. Can't get enough. I'm spring-heeling over the footlights, tearing at his mike.

'You bastards think this is funny? You're all fucked in the head.'

My legs'll hardly carry me. Zig-zagging, jerking arms and legs, out into the night. Into the pub opposite. Jesus, I need a real drink!

Place's deserted but for a couple of guys at a pool table. There's something comforting about the click of billiard balls in a near-empty pub. Over the swaying bar there's a deckle-edged card swimming in and out of focus. '*There are no strangers here, only friends you have not yet met.*' Some destructive smart-ass has crossed out 'strangers' and added 'friends' and vice versa. The landlady stands with her hand on a pump. Everything nice and sane except me, choking with mad rage.

'You look like death warmed up, love. What can I get you? Put hairs on your chest!'

'Brandy. Big one.'

'Have you been over the road? Red Carnation? I'm not surprised you look sick, lovey. Me and my old man skivvied for that mob for years. Down the Walworth Road. He was an election agent. I was filing, making tea. Typing. Then in march the lads in red braces. Mobile phones. Faxes. Downsizing. Out went your clause whatsit and all the faithful old retainers like me and my Les.'

'Yeah. It's bad. The revolution will not be televised, dah, dahdy dah.'

Mirrored behind her bobby-pinned hairdo I see

Tunbridge coming through the door. Immediately I'm wishing I could wave a magic wand and be home, safe and sober on my sofa in front of the telly. He's getting closer. A big, important person. And me, a worm in working class awe.

'Ms Letkin? For what it's worth, I very much support what you did back there. Not many people have the courage to go against the tide. I'm sorry to see an act like that being booked in a Labour Party club. I'll make sure the matter is investigated.'

'Gee, thanks Mr Bainbridge.' What am I thanking him for?

He pushes my glass forward and the landlady instantly refills it.

'And a large Scotch for me,' he says, smiling at the woman behind the bar.

'Looks like the young lady needs cheering up,' she says.

'Well she's just done a very brave thing.'

Dunno what he's on about but he seems friendly. My lips have gone stiff. If I can only get myself together I can tell him all about Trevor and the other bastards. See if he remembers how Mum was beaten up. Tell him about her operation. Weezie and Poojar.

Orson knocks back his drink. His eyes are pale green. When I look into the depths of them I see right into his entrails. A shiver goes down my spine. My maudlin desire to confide evaporates. He bends towards me,

'A little birdie tells me you're very observant, Ms Letkin, and feisty with it. Perhaps too observant and too feisty for your own health.'

Little birdie? What fucking birdie?

'You see, Ms Letkin, not a blade of grass moves in this borough that I don't know about.'

Yes, he remembers my mother. 'She was a bloody nuisance at the time. Caused quite a serious problem for me, disrupting my brilliant career. In fact, it took me two years to fully recover from the damage she did to my reputation. A workmanlike beating was too good for such a stubborn, fixated female.

'Anyway, let's not dwell on the past. I can't tell you how much pleasure it gives me to meet her daughter after all these years and to learn that you have gone over to the enemy, so to speak, working for Gwendoline – or that's how your mother's distorted view of the world sees public servants such as Gwendoline and myself. Oh yes, I imagine your defection from the fold must have reached the parts a thorough bashing couldn't reach. I take my hat off to you, Ms Letkin. Welcome on board, but, remember, watch your step. Others will be watching it for you. I hope you'll remember this conversation when you sober up. Good night to you.' And he walks out.

'Easy come, easy go,' the landlady sighs.

Later. How much later I'll never know. Maybe I was abducted by aliens. The landlady's calling, 'Time, everyone, time. Last orders. Drink up please.'

Where's the car? Did I bring the car? Where the fuck did I park the car? Coins bounce off the floor. I can't tell whether I'm awake or dreaming. On some level I'm using the pub phone to call a cab.

How I got home I don't remember. When I reel in, bouncing off walls, I find Weezie and Poojar tucked up in my king-size and I have to squeeze on to my compact sofa. Mum must be conscious by now, while I'm unconscious. The idea of Mum conscious while I'm unconscious makes me laugh. Soon I'm dreaming. Falling. Crashing. Weezie's standing over me.

'Jesus. What time is it?'
'Five in the morning, Montse. You frightened me.'
'I frightened myself.'

*

Shattered and scared stiff by my half-remembered confrontation with Orson, I wash, dress in office clothes and set off for work. No one's around. The building's deserted. The cleaners have been and gone, leaving the brass fittings glowing and the mirrors clear as open windows. I keep imagining I'm going to bump into Orson and I tremble at my own reflection. A quick whisk with the bug detector is all I can manage today. Not a peep. After what Orson said about me being watched and watching my step, I feel self-conscious, as if I'm not alone, perhaps being overseen by a judgemental stranger and my enjoyment of being in Gwendoline's office is spoiled. At the same time I'm so vulnerable, all alone in this empty place.

I decide on the spur of the minute to ring the hospital. Staff nurse tells me Mum's comfortable. Everything normal. What is normal? Using Gwendoline's accoutrements, I make coffee, wondering what the day will bring.

Orson's scare tactics are working. He probably knows I'm sitting here shitting myself. If I tell Gwendoline how he's been spooking me, she'll only think that somehow I must have given myself away and I'm nothing but an indiscreet blabber, not up to the job. And I called her paranoid! The thing Orson said about me being observant keeps nagging me. What have I observed?

Coffee goes straight through me. In the next-door loo I sit there staring at the tank and sink. Then I focus on a new, innocent-looking piece of ducting over the door. Standing on the bog seat I can just reach. Two screws are all that hold the pieces of flimsy plywood together. I get my knife from my bag and gouge out the screws. Oh boy. Gwendoline's gonna love this. A baby tape recorder. A handwritten card 'Do not disturb' is folded like a place card at a posh dinner. Do not disturb. So I don't.

In my excitement my fears evaporate. I rush next door and ring home. 'Hey, Louise. Sorry to be a pain. Just testing my new phone. Hang on a minute will ya? Don't hang up.' Run to the loo. The tape's spinning merrily. Run back.

'Hey, Louise. Count to ten. Then hang up, right?'

The tape stops the minute Weezie hangs up. Crazy! A grand wasted on crap that can't even detect a fucking tape recorder. So I ring Spymaster to complain. Even though it's not my money, I feel angry. Out of professional curiosity I need to know why the bug alarm wasn't triggered. 'You can't detect recording equipment,' the geezer says. 'Not even when it's attached to a phone?' Not even then, the guy says. 'A bug can only pick up transmitters, something that sends out a signal. Recorders don't send out a signal. If you have a look at the back of the phone you'll see an extra wire coming out . . .'

'Oh yeah, shit!'

My mother's out like a light. No sign of Hughie. So I sit reading the paper. Nothing but bad news. Pope had a heart attack but doctors saved his life.

An apple-cheeked woman in the bed next to Mum keeps trying to engage me in conversation.

'I've had the same thing done as Maria.'

'That's nice.'

'She'll be very uncomfortable for a week or so. I'm just getting over the worst. I'll be going home later. But I still get a lot of wind and it's very painful passing water.'

'I don't want to be rude, but I'm a bit queasy round hospitals. Know what I mean?'

No, she can't take a hint. 'Boil up linseeds for half an hour, strain and drink. A miracle cure for soreness when passing water or doing number twos.'

Mum opens her eyes.

'How you feeling?'

'Montse? Is that you?' Her expression is both pained and painful to see. 'I'm very sore. Quite a lot of bleeding and very uncomfortable flatulence.' Lying here in hospital she's picking up the jargon. Wants to 'evacuate' her bowels instead of 'have a shit' as she normally would.

'Have you been up yet?'

'Not yet. Too sore. Too weak.'

Maybe it's too soon to tell her about my encounter with Tunbridge. Hughie might start his self-righteous shit again if he gets to hear about it. Right now he's had to attend to stuff at the squat where he lives but he could turn up at any minute.

I'd like to offer Mum my place to stay when she comes out. But Weezie's still there. Now she's got her things from Widdecombe she's settled in for the duration. Never mentions Nirvana. When I asked whether he's going to be on the scene she muttered something about karma. Nirvana had told her to accept her lot. Bringing up Poojar on her own was her karma.

'The consultant came round this morning,' Mum says. 'Stuck-up, adulterous little prick. He pressed my stomach, said "very good" and was just going to walk off. So I call out "Wait a minute! What about my sex life."'

'You didn't!' The idea of her sex life repels me.

'Don't make me laugh, Montse. If I laugh it hurts. Stitches. So, I says "when will I be back to normal?" Guess what he says? He says, "Put him in the kennels for a few weeks." What d'you think of that? Put him in the kennels.'

What's normal?

No privacy in here. The woman in the next bed looks as if she's off her skull but she could be feigning sleep for the purpose of eavesdropping. Margaret's still here. Her visitor, dapper, wizened old gent getting a mouthful.

'Why didn't you wear your dacent hat?'

'Because it would have blown away in the wind.'

'You could have put it on t'other way round. How dare you come in here looking like a tramp.'

Ward sister comes along and shouts at the old boy in an ear-splitting voice. The District Nurse has just phoned and wants to know if he's managing all right. 'Would you like her to visit? You can have meals-on-wheels four times a week?'

Margaret bridles up, her eyes glittering. 'He's managing very well, thank you. He doesn't need any visits. He doesn't want the meals-on-wheels.'

'Do you want meals-on-wheels?' The nurse yells, increasing the decibels a peg or two.

'No, I'm all right. I've got me bicycle.'

Mum's been listening. 'It's true,' she says. 'He cycles up here twice a day. God, Montse. I can't stand the petty cruelties in here.'

Margaret has terrible bruising on her left arm and she's unable to bend her right, so the nurses always take her blood pressure over the top of the bruising. Aargh! But I grit my teeth. This is make or break time between me and my Mum. I force myself to remain at her bedside listening to her gruesome tales of patients too weak to lift a fork, silently starving; others turfed out of their beds into a chair so someone more poorly can have a lie down and so on ad nauseam.

Mary, the woman who can't pass urine, cries at night waiting for someone to come and change her bag and then they take forever. Worse when they have to change the catheter. Early this morning, the woman who was in the bed on the other side of Mum discharged herself with a weeping open wound. Had to get home to cook and clean for her husband and kids.

Families. Who'd 'ave 'em!

Talking exhausts Mum and she flops back into a prone

position. 'Why don't you say something for a change? Tell me something to take my mind off my guts.'

Her eyes are closed and her face is relaxed. Seems safe. Where shall I start?

'Gwendoline Rhodes has asked me to do a special job for her. To work for her personally. Every morning for a week I have to go into her office early in the morning and sweep it all over with a bug detector. Before anyone else gets to work. This morning I found a tape recorder hidden behind some ducting in the lavatory next to her office.'

No reaction. Minutes tick by.

'Go on,' Mum says.

Leaning closer, I whisper, 'I'm not supposed to tell anyone. Not even family, Gwendoline said. So don't tell Hughie about this, right?'

Another pregnant pause. Except, in her case, pregnancy is out of the question.

'We'll talk about this again soon, Montse. Maybe in a few days when I'm a bit stronger. I need to rest now. Come back tomorrow, yes?'

'Yeah. See you tomorrow.'

This is fucking amazing! She's talking to me. Even asked me to come back and visit!

Weezie's giving me trouble. When I get back to the flat she wants to know when she can visit Maria. I spout some bull about Maria being bereft of her womanhood. Depressed. Doesn't want to see people. Even though Mum couldn't care less about becoming a wombless wonder. Some women are affected by womb-loss. But I'd like to have all that extraneous stuff removed if only there was a safe and painless way of doing it, like not in a hospital.

Apart from the problem of Weezie's unanswerable questions about my Mum, my job, my life, the universe, I'm definitely on a roll. I'm working directly for Gwendoline now. And I uncovered a secret recording device.

'Hey, Louise. I'm going downstairs to make a few phone calls. The reception's terrible up here on the mobile.'

'Why don't you use the ordinary phone?'

'Because it's work business and I want it charged to my mobile account.'

God, I hate explaining myself to anyone. Explanations and justifications are not my style. I'm getting my folding deck chair out from under the stairs. At the back of the flats there's a communal garden. All the au pairs in the neighbourhood congregate there at lunchtime with their odious little toffs. Poor cows! On closer inspection I see the grass is covered with dog shit. Makes me mad. In a few months Poojar will enjoy crawling about out here. Not easy to find a clear patch to put my chair. If I catch some bastard letting their dog use the place to shit, I'll break their fucking necks.

Down to business, amused to think of the little tape whirring as soon as I dial Gwendoline's number. But there's no reply so the tape doesn't whirr. From where I'm sitting I can see Weezie pottering about in my kitchen and it gives me a nice comforting feeling, knowing she's making lunch for the two of us, Poojar asleep in the Moses basket I bought him. Hell, what am I dreaming of? Domestic bliss?

Try Gwendoline again. Nothing doing. I'm bursting to tell her the news. So I call the main switchboard and ask for Karen.

Snit-face pretends she doesn't know who I am so I have to shout with all the au pairs looking.

'It's me. Montse Letkin. Tenants Relations Officer!'

God, I'm supposed to be on a secret mission here. Might as well use a fucking megaphone. 'Is Gwendoline there?'

'In what regard did you wish to speak with her?'

'Is she there, or not?'

Karen's determined. 'I need to know in what connection you wish to speak with her.'

'It's a personal matter. Er, personal to me, that is. About my compassionate leave.'

'Why don't you speak to your line manager.'

'Because I need to speak to Gwendoline.'

Obviously, Karen thinks I'm some kind of nutter.

five

EVERY FEW HOURS I'M woken by Poojar's kittenish bleating. Being the nice person that I am, and an insomniac, I roll off the sofa to see what's up. 5 a.m. Three more hours and I'm due on the job. In the bedroom Louise has lighted a scented candle. She reclines, incandescently pale. Count Dracula has emptied her veins on a drunken bender. How can she suckle Poojar when she's drained of every drop?

'It's lovely here, Montse,' she says softly. 'Lovely vibes. I'm so grateful to Maria for letting us stay. Have you got any news? When's she coming out of hospital?'

'A few more days yet. When I saw her yesterday she still had trouble getting out of bed on her own.'

Weezie perks up. 'She was always so full of enthusiasm. Remember that time she showed us the labour theory of value using Bryant and May matchsticks? Then she went mad when she saw they were made in Taiwan.'

'Vaguely.'

Clear memory: my mother, elbows on window sill, staring out at the street. Depressed. 'Montse, isn't it strange to think that one day you and I will be gone but those bloody chimney pots will still be there?'

Poojar's making smacking noises with his mouth. Louise shows me how to change his nappy, clean up the mess and apply cream round his tiny purple willie. If only Louise could get a good night's sleep. If anything happens to her, what happens to Poojar?

I'd want to keep him. This pops into my head even though I know nothing about looking after babies. He's a real personality in his own right!

Out of the blue, Louise asks me, 'Where does your name come from, Montse?'

Hazy on that one. 'Some old singer. Sang "Barcelona" with Freddy Mercury. That's all I know.'

'Wow! What a wonderful story.'

'It's not a story. It's a bloody fact!' As usual, whenever my word's doubted, specially if I've juiced things up a bit, I get a triple headrush and palpitations. Tiredness racks up the rage. Worst of it is, I don't even know the true answer to the fucking question. My mother insists on calling herself a citizen of the world. An internationalist. I haven't got a clue where she comes from. Nowhere.

'I didn't mean it like that. Honest, Montse. Don't be so touchy. I think it's great!'

But I *do* know where Letkin comes from. When Mum was confronted with the form to register my birth she decided to name me in honour of Clara Zetkin, Lenin's comrade-in-arms, to whom he wrote letters on The Woman Question.

Z-e-t-k-i-n, Mum wrote in the space for the father's name. But the registrar misread her handwriting and typed L-e-t-k-i-n on my birth certificate. Mum didn't notice till later – Jesus, she couldn't even get *that* right – she was in such a hurry to get out of that stuffy little office. In the discomfort of my naming and shaming, I'd crapped myself. Big time.

'What about *Poo*-jar. What kind of name is that?'

'Oh. It's Indian. A kind of prayer or devotion. An offering to the Goddess or a ceremony. And, Montse . . .'

'Yeah?'

'It isn't *Poo*-jar,' she says quietly, 'it's Puja. I'm not getting heavy, but, you know, it would be nice if you could call him Puja.'

Bugger that. I like it better the other way. I'm not into all that mumbo-jumbo. I'm going back to the sofa.

'Good night, Louise.'

'Buenas noches, Montserrat.'

8.a.m. First person on the ward I see is her, citizen of the world, hobbling along with her toilet bag and towel. Clean nightie over one arm, wheeling a drip with the other, bent over like an old woman.

'Hey, Mum! What are you trying to do?'

'I want a wash.'

Her sweaty nightie could do with changing, I can testify to that. But is this right? Is she allowed to go wandering around on her own?

'Don't look so nervous, Montse. Won't kill me. Just get me to the bathroom.' And I take her elbow awkwardly, hoping I won't have to be there when she undresses.

We manoeuvre ourselves through the door, drip in tow. Not the first time my mother's been attached to a drip.

'How can you have a bath? What about the wound?'

'It's fine if I don't soak it. Just sluice me down.' She sheds her nightie and steps under the shower, flesh perished like an old rubber tyre, pads of it hanging from her drooping shoulders. A thick wad of gauze covers the wound.

'I'm all stapled up, Montse. Instead of stitches they use a staple gun. It's like having a row of safety pins in my gut. Marvellous what they can do these days.'

First I test the water then turn the hose on her. She screws up her face. 'It hurts.'

'If it ain't hurting it ain't working.'

By the time she's patted dry and we've worked out how to get the fresh nightie on without getting tangled up in the drip, she's exhausted and can hardly stand up. 'You better call a nurse,' she growls, slumping on the toilet seat adjusting a monster sanny rag, bigger than one of Puja's nappies.

I yank the communication cord. Five minutes tick by. No help arrives. Mum struggles to her feet, leaning on me heavily. We get through the door.

'You won't believe the way the more ambulant patients stampede in front of you to get to the bathroom,' Mum says. 'I was nearly knocked to the ground when I tried to get up this morning.'

Hughie comes rushing over to us as soon as we show ourselves back on the ward. Tight-lipped, not speaking to each other, the two of us get Mum on her bed. Piss! I was hoping to have some time alone with her so I could tell her about my encounter with Tunbridge. Not that I remember the details. Except that he's back on the scene and he came across the road to the pub to talk to me and it was creepy.

I could tell her that he remembered her. I think she'd be cheered up to know how successful her campaign against him had been and how long it had taken him to stick his head back above the parapet.

Thinking about Orson makes me want to yell, 'Mum, I'm over my head!' She's never there for me when I need her!

'You've worn her out,' Hughie accuses.

'She was already out of bed when I got here. On her way to the bathroom.'

We sit in silence for a few minutes. Mum's snoring. Hughie's sighing.

'Hey, Hughie. D'you know how Mum got her broken hooter?'

He doesn't know. So I tell him the story of the beating she got, throwing in a few extra details of my own ordeal. How she put me through it for the sake of the revolution.

He says, 'Maybe Maria was right. It was a mistake on my part getting you involved with her again, Montse. You're a disruptive influence. You're only concerned with yourself and your own needs. You couldn't care less about your mother. She needs all her strength to get better. You come in here and upset her.'

What's the bastard talking about? I haven't been upsetting her. We've been getting along fine.

'Is that what she said?'

'No. I'm saying it. You've been telling her all sorts of off-the-wall stuff. What you're doing for Gwendoline Rhodes. And it upsets her. You're either disturbed in the head or you're in a lot of trouble. Either way, she doesn't need it right now.'

'Mum! Do you hear what he's saying?'

She doesn't respond so I'm leaning over to give her a nudge when Hughie catches my wrist in a vice-like grip. 'Don't push it, Montse. Do your mother a favour, leave now.'

Hughie wins. I have to leave. I'm not letting that fucking great queen see me cry.

Outside the hospital a bus comes along that takes me straight down the office. My car's missing. I've combed the streets for blocks near the Red Carnation and it wasn't in the spot where I thought I left it, so for the moment I'm using the integrated (disintegrated, more like) public transport system. Little things like a bus turning up exactly when I need it make my day. By the time I've crossed the lobby in the town hall, my problem with Hughie's back in perspective.

It's a closed world in the council building. Bunkered. Not many workers to be seen. In spite of nervous jokes about the proletariat staying indoors playing with their nintendoes, you can smell the constant paranoid fear that the unemployed or the homeless might magically materialise *en masse* in a threatening role. Perhaps skateboarding in from ghettoes. Or they may attack silently, swiftly and undetected. No slogans, no parties, no unions.

9.30 a.m. Monday morning. Routine day. I've left the Spymaster equipment hidden in the flat, pending further orders. This stage of my work for Gwendoline is over. All that's left is to make my report. Should I approach her? Or wait for her to call me? I can't bear sitting around like a spare prick at a wedding. I like to be proactive. Will she believe me when I tell her I saw Stan going into those toilets? No one else was present, I'm sure, but now it dawns on me — what Orson meant about me being observant — somehow he knows I saw Stan. I need to consult my chief.

As I've got a bit of time up my sleeve, I'm taking a chance on catching Gwendoline in her office. Top floor's deserted. Cleaners been and gone. Big pile of mail on Karen's desk. No Karen. Having a sort through I see foreign stamps, junk mail, registered packets tied up with bits of string, handwritten envelopes pathetically penned by imploring, quaking hands and a few post-marked 'House of Commons' which I guess are from MPs going through the motions of taking up cases for constituents.

Something tweaks the corner of my eye, something glinting on the floor halfway between the desk and the curtained balcony. I rush across and grasp a fat, gold watch. Gwendoline's Rolex. Holding the thing in my hand, heavy as a manacle, I experience the pulsating glow of Gwendoline's charisma embedded in the warm metal.

Vinnie greets me by the coffee machine, baring his needle-sharp teeth. 'God, Montse. You were loaded the other night. You frightened Sikowits out of his wits. Geddit?'

'Don't remember much about it.' Gwendoline's watch is biting achingly into the flesh of my forearm.

'Know what people're saying? They're saying you missed the irony.'

'What fucking irony? You mean, the card up the sleeve of art?'

Now he's shouting. 'It's supposed to shock. It gets people to face up to their own bigotry!'

'If they've just discovered what fucking arseholes they are, what the fuck are they laughing at?'

Vinnie stares. 'You're a bloody head case. You know that, Montse? A bloody head case.'

But I'm invincible. Protected by the armour of a higher being: Gwendoline.

'Fuck you, Vinnie.'

Off he goes, muttering into his coffee. Vinnie thinks it's smart to hand out unwanted advice. One time he told me I shouldn't come in the office wearing the threads I wear on the street. Pollutes the atmosphere. Told me right to my face I stank. As if I didn't know. In my line of work you have to mix with some dirty fuckers and you need to blend in. An occupational hazard.

Roger calls the team into his office, looking pleased with himself. 'Nice to have you back with us,' he says to me, sarkily. Maureen mouths, 'How's your mum?' Roger begins to say some smart-arse thing about me not being able to handle my drink, how my little outburst at the Red Carnation proved what a bleeding heart I was underneath my cocky exterior, when a siren starts shrieking in the street outside.

'You made an exhibition of yourself the other night.' I pretend I can't hear. Then I can't. He gives up. More sirens join in. It's getting louder and louder. Over the top of this cacophony he's trying to tell us his budget's been increased. Four more full-time, trained investigators are being taken on. They'll be needed to cover the extra work caused by the national fraud hotline. Change is in the air. Lots more work pouring into the office, Roger says.

Before the election huge hoardings had gone up all over the country encouraging civic-minded citizens to phone the National Fraud Hotline and dob in their neighbours and friends. At first Roger'd been worried that the new government might scrap the fraud line before he had a chance to implement his grandiose plans for our department. But all was well, the fraud line stayed and thrives. Matters pertaining to local authorities are still being referred from them to us. Ain't been so much telephonic activity since the Squidgy tapes.

The sirens subside but continue their intermittent whelping. On the subject of more staff, Maureen's blank. Kenny and Mike are suspicious.

'Will we have to share our office space?' Kenny says. He's afraid his extra-curricular activities might be discovered. Jerk doesn't realise, everyone knows he sits there all day reading Marvel comics on the net. They go on asking their stupid questions. If I was staying in the department I'd feel pissed off that a bunch of curtain-twitching amateurs will be horning in on our act. Fucking joke! It's Maureen I feel sorry for. She hates change. Meeting new people. Why should I care? Not that I don't care deeply about the human race. It's people I can't stand. Soon I'll be well out of it, doing the new job Gwendoline's got lined up for me. Maybe I can take Maureen with me? Do her a favour. She ain't got much up top but she's loyal. Do anything I asked her.

We're all sitting on our arses wondering about our futures when there's an announcement over the tannoy.

'Due to a security alert the police have requested that nobody leaves the building until further notice.' I look at Gwendoline's watch. Ten fifteen.

'Fuck's going on?' Roger grabs his phone and tries to raise the operator.

Maureen, who hardly ever contributes anything to a conversation, practically makes a speech.

'It might be the IRA,' she opines. 'One time, in Marks, there was this announcement. "Mr Green is in the store." I told the girl at the check-out "that's code for a bomb scare". The whole place cleared in five seconds.'

Mike says, 'If it is a bomb, they won't tell us. When I was in security, staff were always last to know.'

For once I agree with Roger, 'They've asked us not to leave the building,' he says. 'If it was a bomb, they'd evacuate the place.' He orders us to get back to our desks and write up any outstanding reports. Prat's antsy and I know why. Later this morning there's a raid on a dodgy landlord. Hype's been going on for months. Roger's going in with a television crew. Documentary. Good PR. Busting evil landlords. Selfish little fucker always keeps the plum jobs for himself. Jeez, I can hardly wait to get shot of him.

Back at my desk, I ring Gwendoline's office. No answer. Most times Karen picks up the phone at this time of day or the answerphone kicks in. Now neither is happening.

And I can't wait to tell Gwendoline about my debugging success story. Plus, literally up my sleeve, I have the added bonus of having found her watch.

Frustrated, I ring the hospital. Mum's 'comfortable'. I try Gwendoline's office a few more times, then I ring home. Weezie sounds tired but otherwise OK. Says she might go out for a while.

'Anything special you'd like me to get for dinner?' I inquire, hoping to deflect her from going out, possibly to Widdecombe Hall. 'Just tell me what you want and I can do a shop on my way home.' But she says she needs to stretch her legs. Get some fresh air.

'Turn up the ironiser. That'll freshen up the air!' Makes me nervous, her going out. If she learned the truth about my job, it wouldn't be the end of the world. But I'm wound up. Claustrophobic. Told I can't leave the building, I badly want out.

Maureen beckons me to the window. Blue lights flashing down below. Rows of cop cars, an ambulance, even a fire engine. Cops are looping orange tape between the pavement and road. 'What could it be?' Maureen whispers.

Now Roger's standing in the middle of the room, face putty-coloured, jowls quivering like he's going to throw up.

'Can I have your attention please.' Bastard's talking like a tannoy. 'I've just heard. There's been a fatal accident. Apparently, Gwendoline Rhodes has fallen from her balcony. She's been killed. The police will be coming round during the day. You can go and get coffee from the machine. But don't go far. Certain parts of the building are being cordoned off. Don't attempt to cross the police tape.'

Pins and needles in my head. Icy mush inside. I see Gwendoline falling, her body turning over and over in the sky like a stick person. Then I blank out.

Shouting.

'Montse! You fainted.'

Maureen's forcing scalding tea between my lips. Oh, thanks guys. They've laid me out on a desk with my legs in the air. Waves of nausea sweeping over me.

'Get the nurse,' Roger orders.

'I'm OK.' I try to sit up. 'What's the time? How long have I been out?'

'Half ten,' Maureen says. 'You was only out for a few minutes.'

'Is it real?' I ask her. 'Did someone just say Gwendoline's dead?'

Maureen nods. 'It's been a shocker.'

'I'm scared of heights,' I try to explain my extreme reaction. 'The thought of falling's enough to give me a bad turn.'

In the background, Roger's barking out instructions. 'All right everyone. Fun's over. Get back to your desks.'

He hovers over me. 'Take it easy for a while. Put your head between your knees.'

I'm operating on two levels of consciousness. Numbing shock, with sickening imaginings of the exact moment when Gwendoline hit the pavement and, behind that, a calculating detachment. The full import of Gwendoline's death is sinking in and a little voice inside asks how it's going to affect me, Montse Letkin. What about the new job she promised me? What about Mum's new flat? The injustice annihilates me. No Gwendoline, no promotion. No re-housing for Mum.

After remarkably few minutes the whispers start. 'Did she fall or was she pushed?'

Gwendoline Rhodes was a woman with the interpersonal skills of Enver Hoxha, so disliked and feared everyone fantasised about topping her. But in the end, when it seems she's done it all on her own, we're thunderstruck. Can't take it in. An indestructible thing has been destroyed!

Kenny and Mike, pretending not to be awed, giggle nervously, exchanging Gwendoline jokes. 'Once she was bitten by a serpent. The serpent died.'

According to the whispers, the council stands to pay out grands and grands if Gwendoline croaks it on the job. Anything happens to her at work, her dependants collect the jackpot. Unless it's suicide, which is what is being assumed for the moment.

'Shakespeare, or was it Oscar Wilde?' Roger isn't sure. Both, I think. 'Whoever said we all kill the thing we love most was wrong. Think about it! Gwendoline would never kill the thing she loved most: herself!'

Gwendoline's job, if you strip away the trimmings, was to keep the lid on things. And in so doing she acquired hundreds, if not thousands, of ill-wishers and enemies. Maybe she never thought about the hatred she incurred, sitting up there in her ivory tower. Maybe she just didn't think. People can turn nasty when they get stitched up over key money, or a contract goes to a business rival. Even yuppies feel the rage when they can't pay their mortgages and their BMWs are repossessed. If you're a prick, do you not bleed?

Gwendoline was a high flier in the Labour Party, no doubt seeing herself as the future Dowager Lady Rhodes, farting into ermine. The chairman of British Nuclear Fuels had had the call, the British Airways boss had had the call, other local government tyros, even lowly little policy wonks who'd worked for Gwendoline in the past had had the call. But still her telephone did not ring.

High flier? Did I say high flier? The lunchtime newscaster reads out her name in full on the office telly. Gwendoline Amelia Earhart Rhodes. Jesus Christ! Flap your wings and fly to daddy. I bet she wished she could fucking fly this morning.

She was pushworthy. I won't argue with that. But in retrospect I always thought, like everybody else, that Gwendoline was unpushable. Who would dare? No matter how tantalisingly she teetered on the brink of falling, the onlooker, however heartfelt the desire to be rid of her, would rather rush to pluck her from the jaws of death than run the risk of her surviving to point the finger and extract a horrible revenge. The tongue-lashings she meted out to those foolish enough to speak against her in the council chamber were enough to reduce strong men to tears. No way, Josie: seeing her go overboard with my own eyes would not be reassurance enough for yours truly. Inevitably, on the way down there would be a life-saving awning or a hay-cart piled high, parked underneath, on which she would make a soft landing. And then, the accusations, the deadly retribution.

Style your way out of that one, baby! Even if she was shoved, there was no guarantee the cow would fall down. Our Gwendoline was diamond-shaped: sleek little head, sloping shoulders, wide flat hips, tapering down to dainty feet rooted on terra firma. Her body quivered with rootedness like a dagger hurled into floorboards. If pushed, she would twang back upright.

That's what we all thought. Wrongly. When pushed, as I intuit, she did not spring into the vertical position like a Russian doll, nor did she miraculously land in an awning, nor sink luxuriously into piled up hay. She hit the pavement like the ten-stone woman she was.

I'm not party to what goes on in the corridors of power. All I know is, there's an eerie, half-expectant silence in the halls which lately echoed with the lively clatter of Gwendoline's stilettoes. The atmosphere is totally electric.

Rumour chases counter-rumour as we await our visit from the twos 'n blues.

Four DCs are interviewing over three hundred of us. Gwendoline's Rolex is weighting me down, pushed as far up my arm as it will go. First they come round and take names. One by one we're summoned for questioning. Time to cogitate. *Tempus fugit* painfully slowly. They're using the grand committee room, scene of Gwendoline's greatest triumphs. The room shrieks with her presence. The coppers are two men and two women. Hooray for equality! DC Chiang calls my name. Hair black as a raven's wing, fingernails recently trimmed, the man's clean as a whistle, sweet-smelling and gorgeous. His questioning is far from taxing. I scan the faces of the other policemen who come up to whisper, cupping their hands around one of his perfect shell-like ears. Then they mince away on tiptoe. Death makes people whisper, speak in sepulchral voices and walk on tiptoe. Even the Beast.

As far as the gavvers are concerned I've never even met Gwendoline personally. So there's not much for me to say. I'm confident she told no one of our arrangement. I told, er, hardly anyone. Only my mother. Did Mum tell Hughie? Yes, she must have said something to Hughie.

I spell out my name, age, date of birth, how long I've worked for the council, my job title. DC Chiang doesn't ask me what a Tenants Relations Officer actually does. Even when I hint, 'So, we're sort of in the same line of business.' No response. He keeps his eyes averted, concentrating on writing in his notebook. Perhaps he already knows what a Tenants Relations Officer does. What time did I arrive at work this morning? Did I notice anything strange? Had I ever met Gwendoline? I press my forehead.

'A couple of times. Only briefly. Never alone.'

DC Chiang writes it down.

'When was the last time you saw her?'

Making it so precise bothers me. Prevarication's easier when things are left vague.

'To be honest, I can't remember. Probably at a meeting of the whole department when she announced the latest policy initiative.' He writes.

'When can I go home?'

'We apologise, Ms Letkin, but we can't allow any one person to leave until everybody has been questioned. It's a matter of routine. We are sorry for the inconvenience.'

'What happened? Did she fall or was she pushed?'

'We're keeping an open mind at the moment. Thanks, Ms Letkin. Can you ask Miss Maureen Simpson to come in?'

We're still there at 8 o'clock in the evening. Starving. All we've got to eat are canteen sandwiches, damp white blotting paper filled with dry, curling cheese. Crap tea and coffee. I feel cruddy inside. Why, oh why, oh why won't they let us nip out to the deli? Jesus, they've got everyone's names and addresses. We can't leave town without them knowing.

Just when all our nerves are stretched to breaking point, there's an announcement. We can go. Weirdest thing is, we're reluctant to part and depart. People hanging around the lobby, talking in hushed tones. I'm looking everywhere for Stan. No one's seen him. Did he tell the cops about his bugging activities? A bunch of people are going to the pub to wind down. Stan's not in the pub either. I'm going looking for him.

As I emerge from the tube at Brixton a man asks me politely if I've finished with my travelcard. He'll resell it for 50p. For some reason I hand it over. Outside the station a gospel group are singing their hearts out for the Lord. Takes all sorts.

Stan lives in a pleasant terrace behind Olive Morris House. The door bursts open when I ring. An angry woman I take to be Mrs Stan begins berating me. 'You can keep him for all I care. I'm leaving him. Orson's got him running round in circles. He spends more time with that jumped-up prat than he does with me. If you want him you can have him.'

Stan's missus is taking a lot of persuading that I certainly don't want Stan in the way that she thinks. Far from it. I only want to talk to him, all the more urgently, now his wife's confirmed his connection with Orson.

The hallway's chocka with cardboard boxes and signs of frantic packing. She means business. A child's demanding voice keeps calling, 'Mum, Mum!'

'Shuddup!'

She waves her hand at a tattered poster on the wall right by the door, greeting visitors. Some sort of trade union demo with hundreds of little figures like pegs making up a sea of marchers carrying banners inscribed 'Remember Grunwick' with hundreds of other tiny pegs in police uniform.

'See that? That was Stan before he went rotten. Now it's yes Orson, no Orson, three bags full Orson, pager bleeping all hours of the night. He keeps telling me it's all going to be over soon. But I'm sick of it. Can't wait any longer. I'm leaving him.' By the end of the speech she's nearly sobbing. I back away and she slams the door.

By the time I get home it's all hours. Louise is fast asleep with Puja lying on her stomach, watchful as a cat, eyes shining under his green, gold and black crocheted hat.

'You were late last night,' Weezie says. I don't even flinch when she cross-questions me. We're like an old married couple now, me holding the paper up in front of my face as she serves hash browns and eggs.

'Any coffee?'

Gwendoline's demise has made the home news pages.

'Coffee coming up. Oh, by the way, Montse. Don't use the milk in the glass jug in the fridge. I've expressed four ounces so Puja can try feeding from a bottle at night sometimes. You could even feed him yourself occasionally, if you felt like it.'

'What do you mean, "expressed"?'

'You use a breast pump. The milk comes out. You collect it. Refrigerate it. Then someone else can do the feeding once in a while. Just to give me a rest.'

'Yuk! I could have put that in my coffee!'

'If you did, it wouldn't do you any harm. You're so tetchy this morning, Montse. What's the matter with you? Is it another hangover?'

Where to start? What's really bugging me is the bug. Supposing the police find it and hear me ringing Weezie? Hear her counting to ten and me fiddling with the phone?

'Someone died at work yesterday. It was a stresser.'

Weezie looks concerned. As I'm telling her, imagining the mechanics of the fall, Gwendoline on the parapet, stepping out into nothingness, I come out in a cold sweat again. Droplets spring out on my forehead and trickle down my face like tears.

'Montse, you're not well.'

'Look!' I fold the newspaper into a square with the picture of Gwendoline uppermost for Weezie to see. She takes it and reads.

'I work in the Town Hall. I told you that, didn't I?'

'No. You did not.'

Now I've started, I can't shut it. 'I do secret work. For the council. Getting evidence against bastards who racially harass their neighbours. Stuff like that. This flat belongs to me, not my mother. I just felt awkward, knowing how you feel about people owning property. Especially you being in a hostel. Know what I mean? It seemed out of order to mention it.'

Weezie looks doubtful.

'Thank you for being so sensitive, Montse.'

Is she taking the pee? 'But I still don't understand. Do you think I'm so judgemental? I always try my best not to judge anyone.'

'I made a mistake, Weezie. It was a spur of the moment thing. I didn't want you to feel awkward so I said the stuff about this being Mum's place. Are we still mates?'

Frowning sternly, she nods.

After getting that off my chest, I decide to call the office and tell them I'll be late today. I need to find my wheels.

six

I'D BEEN WALKING RIGHT by without even recognising my own vehicle! Nearside window's stove in, Dalston diamonds scattered all over the front seat, and there's a great gaping lacuna where my stereo used to be. My motor's clamped, covered in grime and gob and the boot's been attacked with a giant tin-opener. Won't close properly. Final insult: some tosser's stuck a note on the windscreen saying, 'Thank you for ruining our weekend with your car alarm.' The more I glare at the wreckage, the madder I am.

When I get on the mobile to call up the insurance company, the manager's too busy to speak to me. Keep ringing him every five minutes, going ballistic standing in the street with the phone stuck to my ear like a limpet. The calm breathing Weezie's been trying to teach me ain't working.

A blue Fiesta wiggles up to the yellow line. DC Chiang calls out cheerily. What the fuck is he doing here?

'Hullo, I saw you there. You look distressed. Can I help?'

He hops out and stands on the pavement looking at my car with a pained expression.

'This is a bit more than casual vandalism, don't you

think? Someone's made a serious effort to get into your boot. Did you have anything valuable in there?'

He kicks the tyres as if he's thinking of buying them for scrap. Gets down and peers underneath.

'Not a very neat clamping job,' he says like a connoisseur, 'must be one of those cowboy outfits. If you want, we can drive up and down a few streets. Look for the clamping unit. See if we can get some action.'

DC Chiang has rescued me. The breathing's calmed down. I put my phone away. He chats in a relaxed friendly fashion as we bowl along. Says he's been looking for me at the office. An incident room's been set up *in situ* and he wanted to talk to me some more.

'Howja know where to find me?'

He shrugs. All he had to do was ring my flat. My friend said I was out looking for my car.

'It was a simple matter to get your registration number and check it out on the computer. I drove by on the off chance you were here. And you were.'

'That's a lot of trouble to go to.'

Every time there's a clear stretch of road he puts his foot down and if it wasn't for the seat belt I'd be flying through the windscreen. The jerky stop-start driving's scary and sick-making.

'There was something I wasn't quite clear about,' he says, jumping a red light. 'When I get a bee in my bonnet I have to deal with it right away, before it becomes an irritant. You told me you never saw Ms Rhodes alone at any time. Is that right?'

He punctuates this by jumping straight over a culvert like a pursuit driver, rattling my teeth.

During our interview it had been a matter of course to tell him as little as possible. Think before speaking!

'What with the shock 'n all, I forgot. Now I remember,

I did see her one time. She called me in to give me a bollocking over a work-related matter.'

At this speed, I'm unable to focus my anxiety. My vehicle's been trashed and I'm bouncing up and down in a cop car with my mouth running. What did I think of Gwendoline? How did I find her to work with? Why ask me? I hardly knew the woman. Where did he get the idea I might be able to add something to his pool of information? Maybe he's another one who's keen on the grain-of-sand theory of human progress.

Anyway, here goes.

'For what it's worth, in my opinion she was the sort of person who wouldn't sit down to shit unless she had a velvet loo seat. But I don't know why you're asking me. We had nothing in common. There was no reason for our paths to cross.'

'And yet you knew her son?'

The man's doo-lally. Gwendoline didn't have kids. In fact, I can't think of anything weirder than Gwendoline with a kid. No way Josie. We screech up to a give-way sign.

'You were noticed in his company at a social event. According to various people we've talked to, the two of you were head to head most of the evening.'

The same big mouths must've told him I'd had a skinful that night. Can't remember, Jack. Must've been going round talking to all kinds of people, taking names and giving out my particulars to anyone I took a fancy to. Later on I'd looked through the small notebook I always keep in my pocket. A couple of torn out sheets confirms that I was dishing out my phone number. Two pages ripped out means two people may be walking round with my particulars on their person. Whether or not I was able to write down my number legibly is another matter.

'I don't remember much about the other night,' I confess

to DC Chiang. 'As far as I know, Gwendoline didn't have kids. But I'm just assuming. She might have had half a dozen for all I know. I didn't know her outside of work.'

He slows the car. Up ahead is the van we've been looking for. I have to fork out £100 on the spot. Chiang drops me back at my car where I cool my heels for half an hour before the bastards come and release their Detroit boot.

Since Gwendoline went to the great one-stop-shop in the sky, I'm discombobulated. Wrong-footed at every turn. First I tell the cops I never saw Gwendoline alone, then I change my story, deny knowing Gwendoline's son, then remember Billy the kid, the wacky little guy at the Labour club. Is Billy Gwendoline's son? Even worse, DC Chiang has spoken to Weezie. How do I wangle my way out of that? I need to sort my head out.

The tough mental effort of retrieving Billy from the murky depths of my beer-soaked brain causes him to magically reappear. Back at the flat, after a do-nothing day at work, confirmation of his actual existence is here — a long, rambling message monopolising the whole tape on my answer machine. Talking as if I'm a close, bosom buddy, telling me all his business. Fixated with his mother. Yet another minor cause of major freak-out for Weezie.

'I get a creepy vibe from his voice, the way he rambles and obsesses. Keep away from him, Montse, the guy's trouble. He's got no boundaries.'

'Nah, he's harmless.'

Weezie and Puja are asleep in the bedroom. Resentfully, I dial the out-of-town number he's left. He's in a terrible state. 'Get a grip,' I tell him.

'The police keep going on about Gwendoline making all sorts of trips back and forward to the Scilly Isles. They keep asking me. As far as I know she's never even been there. I don't even know where the fucking place is. What should I tell them? Please come and see me, will you, Montse?'

His Granny's catatonic. But, from what Billy says, that's nothing new. And the press have been bothering them, popping up on the doorstep at all hours trying to get pictures. Now Gwendoline's dead the media have cast her as a fallen star, a future Mayor of London.

Right this minute all I care about is getting Billy off the phone. I agree to go and see him. Then I tell him, 'Don't ring me again leaving long, rambling messages. You freaked out my flatmate!'

DC Chiang presses the green button and starts recording. 'Interview with Ms Montse Letkin, 10.30 a.m. on Monday 10th with WPC Cattermole in attendance.' Then he beams at me. 'Now, Ms Letkin, I've requested this meeting because we understand that everyone needed to take a little bit more time to absorb the initial shock of what's happened. We wondered if, on reflection, you might be able to help us after all?'

'Well,' I say, carefully. 'You're right. I've been thinking about events leading up to Gwendoline's death and I've come up with a few things which might prove to be of significance. See, Gwendoline had sworn me to secrecy. The fact is, I was working for her. Performing tasks which only I could be entrusted with. None of her colleagues knew she'd taken me on as her personal assistant. In the aftershock, I was still thinking about confidentiality. I hadn't digested the fact that Gwendoline wasn't going to come back.'

DC Chiang looks at me encouragingly. 'Ah, yes. A common phenomenon. Please go on, Ms Letkin.'

'Acting on the personal instructions of Ms Rhodes, I

purchased an anti-bugging device. She asked me to use the aforementioned device to sweep her office every day before she started work. She told me someone was out to get her. That's why she needed me on the case. As a trained investigator.'

WPC Cattermole's vicious eyes give her mean little thoughts away. I rage at her.

'Don't look at me like that! You'll be smirking on the other side of your ugly mug in a minute. I can demonstrate beyond any doubt that what I'm telling you is true. I found a tape recorder, hidden in the women's toilet adjacent to Gwendoline's office.'

DC Chiang nods soothingly. 'Excellent,' he says. 'Very helpful.'

He wants dates. I think back. Using my hospital visits as a benchmark, it isn't difficult to work out. And, bloody Ada! I nearly forgot Stan. On hearing about Stan the Man's little visit to the lavatory, the detective assumes a serious expression.

'You say you saw Stan at what time? Can you describe what he was wearing?'

All of which information I happily supply.

The DC's finger is poised above the off button: 'Interview with Ms Letkin concluded at 10.55 a.m. WPC Cattermole and myself are now accompanying Ms Letkin to find the evidence she has spoken about.'

I experience a *frisson* of excitement and terror as Cattermole lifts the yellow tape for me to climb under; permission to enter forbidden territory, coupled with close proximity to the place where Gwendoline Rhodes gasped her last.

We dovetail into the space by the basins as I point out the overhead ducting where the recorder is to be found. DC Chiang produces a useful blade from an inside pocket and, mounting the edge of the lavatory bowl, reaches up and loosens the plywood casing.

But the cupboard is bare. WPC Cattermole sucks her teeth and smiles meanly. DC Chiang replaces the piece of wood and steps down. He clears his throat, faintly apologetic, and looks at the floor.

'P'rhaps somebody got here before us?'

seven

MUM'S MOVED INTO Hughie's squat which is nowhere near as comfortable as my place but, of course, she doesn't know how nice my place is, so she's quite happy. But there's no escaping the smell of formaldehyde. Of all places, the squat's in an old hospital. Mum's installed in a smartly painted room where her dog-eared SCUM and Communist Manifestos frottage together on a hastily erected bookshelf. From the platform of a massive double futon inadequately covered by a big lumpy duvet, she presides in a sickeningly matriarchal manner over a gaggle of young crusties. In return for sharing the same space as a wise woman and imbibing her words of wisdom they bring her environmentally-friendly carrot and coriander soup – which they have on tap – with chunks of bread you need a block and tackle to lift to your mouth.

'You young people have given me fresh hope. I used to despair of the next generation. . . .' I catch her saying on my first visit. When she claps her mincers on me the sentence trails away.

'Hospital's like being in the trenches,' she says, acting the conquering shero. 'Blood, shit and tears. You're lucky to get out alive!'

Mum wants to talk about the after-effects of her

operation and I want to talk about me for a change. One of the things I hate about sick people is that they only want to talk about themselves all the time.

'I can't sleep,' she moans, 'my shoulder hurts, my pee's cloudy, and I have to get up two or three times in the night. Rich food makes me queasy and I'm knackered after walking a few yards.'

Her devotees, who've never suffered anything more serious than a grazed knee between them, murmur appreciatively. Oh yeah, an underclass shero is something to be. Her followers gape, wince and swoon as she proudly displays her wound with its proud flesh. And they always come back for more, even when she's rude. One of them picks up a book and asks, 'Maria, may I borrow this?'

'What do you think this is? A public library!' she snaps and the poor cow returns the book to the shelf and slinks away in disgrace.

Maria hasn't asked me about Gwendoline and it occurs to me she might not have heard about our massive drama down the council. I don't see a TV or radio in here and nobody reads newspapers. The inhabitants of this place get their information on a hierarchical need-to-know basis exactly like the regime at the town hall. Here, Maria's top of the hierarchy. Where does she get her information? She would say that she doesn't need to be told anything or read anything because she's been around for so long that there's nothing in the world that she hasn't heard before. But if she hasn't yet heard of Gwendoline's death I'm happy to be the one to tell her. See if I can surprise her for once.

'These staples are coming out tomorrow,' she announces, exposing her belly. 'Who's coming to the GP with me?'

'I will, I will,' they chorus like I-am-Spartacus. Why didn't she ask me? Ain't I her nearest and dearest?

Then she shoos them out and they go, casting reluctant backward glances at their guru. A reserved silence falls between us now we're alone, the two of us sat here like a pair of lemons just looking at each other. Then she says, 'I've been waiting to hear what you've got to say about Gwendoline's death. I thought you'd've turned up earlier to fill me in on the gory details.'

Which I do, unable to resist embellishing here and there and playing up my own role in the affair. Maria's face is hard to read. She may be disbelieving things which actually did happen, like me working on a special job for Gwendoline, and believing some of the slight reshaping of events, such as me giving the impression that I'd been working for Gwendoline for longer than I actually did.

'I don't like the idea of you being questioned by the filth,' she growls. 'I don't like that at all. I hope you didn't spin them one of your yarns. You could land yourself in a lot of trouble.'

'But, Mum, I didn't tell them anything!'

'What's to tell?'

Maria goes apeshit when I remind her about the anti-bugging. First she accuses me of fantasising – what can I do to convince her? I'm holding back the matter of the disappearing tape recorder, still smarting from the humiliation of that empty space. I offer to go home and bring the Spymaster equipment to show her. She declines my offer. I'm fingering Gwendoline's watch beneath my sleeve, dying to show it off, as Maria puts me through the third degree. Wants to know more about Orson, exactly what he does for the council, what he said to me, have the police questioned him too?

'If what you tell me is true, and I'm not accusing you of lying, so don't go into one ... if what you say is true, then you need to get yourself prepared for next time the pigs decide to grill you. Don't go pitching them any wild tales about working for Gwendoline, geddit? Don't give them the chance to fit you up with anything.

'Go and see my old comrade, Matthew. He worked closely with Gwendoline in the 70s. Ever since she went rotten, he's followed her career and kept tabs on every political manoeuvre she's made. He'll give you background to help you to get a better grasp of what's going on.'

Sounds like that's the sort of material that DC Chiang would like to get his hands on. But I'll go and see Matthew alone.

'Pass me that file.' Mum's pointing to the bookshelf where there's a box file stuffed with old leaflets from demos and meetings going back years. 'Matthew brings out an occasional newsletter. If I can find one, his address will be at the bottom.'

Just the smell of Mum's file is enough to flood my mind with memories of her sitting up all night photocopying and sticking up papers with cow gum; using Letraset, steel ruler and Stanley knife, to produce articles which were circulated only to a tiny circle of people whom she considered 'good comrades'. Throwing money away on postage to addresses where houses had been demolished to make way for urban development and, even at my tender age, I imagined her tracts lying unopened until eventually disposed of with the rest of the unsolicited junk mail; schemes to make your fortune, you've been chosen from 650,000 names etc., offers of fabulous prizes and ball-breaking loans.

By and by a political landscape has arisen which is barely recognisable to my mother, despite her efforts to keep up with the yoof of today. I almost feel it would be cruel to tell her: unknown to her the things that people want to protest about have shifted shape behind her back. Labour aristocracy has taken on a whole new meaning from the days when union barons commanded the Labour Party. The new Labour aristocracy are City tycoons, bankers, financiers, supermarket millionaires and futures traders. Some are the real McCoy! Yes, the landed and loaded are depositing their dynastic derrières on Labour's Benches in the Lords, calling for constitutional reform along lines acceptable to their class.

'After all's said and done, we're not living in the 19th century, are we old chap?'

But Maria isn't interested in examining the entrails of bourgeois democracy. She's an all-or-nothing woman!

Before even meeting him I visualise Matthew as the kind of old-style comrade Maria might still be if she hadn't belatedly discovered feminism, fallen in with the crusties and decided to try her luck as a new age matriarch. All the same, I will pay Matthew a visit. Like Maria says, for my own protection I need to know much more about the kind of people I'm dealing with. And she learned the hard way. Evidence of past naiveté is sculpted on her face.

Dozens of doorbells labelled with flat numbers but no names, which is his? Standing in the freezing cold, I'm wondering what to do, when out comes the Hulk on speed, another great tub about to drop a bundle, and I get my chance. Slip in behind her and she doesn't even notice. Clambering over a pile of prams in the hall, I'm hit bang in the face with a cloud of solvent fumes. Pah! You can't help breathing it in. Choking piss and glue. And now I see what's causing it. On the bottom stair, two bulky shapes. Heads shorn, swastika tats, scabby fingers clutching cans of special brew. Hand-cuffed together.

Getta loada those eyes. Whatever they're on makes smack look homeopathic!

'Where yer from?'

'Here.'

'Yer don' look it.'

'Can I pass please, mate?'

'Where yer parents from?'

'Here.'

'Yer don' look it. Oy, this is my fiancé. AWOL from over the water. They cuffed us but we got away.'

'Nice one.'

Both are built like brick shithouses. I'm edging my way through the pong and they're not trying to stop me.

Upstairs the odour of sour laundry and bad plumbing seems fragrant as a rose by comparison.

At the top of the house Matthew's name is sellotaped to a door on a yellowed strip of paper. A line of sand-blasted milk bottles stands against the wall covered in cobwebs and dust, a heap of burnt-out aluminium kettles, undisturbed for years by the looks of it. The long-remembered clacking of an old-fashioned typewriter causes a strange nostalgia to creep over me, reviving further buried memories of my mother, sweating over her yawn-making tracts.

When I knock the clattering instantly stops and unwelcoming vibes radiate from the crack under the door. Then the typing resumes. Nervously straining for sounds of movement I bang again and hear chains being rattled, bolts and latches sliding. The door opens half an inch and a reedy baritone commands,

'Speak!'

'Matthew Maloney?'

'Who wants to know?'

I insert one of my specially printed cards into the opening. Knobbly fingers snatch.

'I'm the daughter of Maria De Mesquita.'

The door gives way.

Sunspokes jab through a small high window on the

other side of the room, piercing my eyes in a disorientating fashion.

As I step into the room I can't find a place for my feet to go. Every inch of floor is covered with stacks of papers, books, magazines, cuttings, notes, index cards, cashier's receipts, betting slips, transport dockets, old bus tickets. By the wall, a narrow folding bed, a small table with a typewriter on it and, at the epicentre of this highly inflammable material, a pyromaniac's dream, a tall, narrow oil heater giving off a sputtering, noxious flame. In the corner, a sink and gas ring.

I make out a sofa half-buried in mountains of paper.

'Sit!' Matthew commands, filling a blackened aluminium kettle from the tap. Bag of bones in a blue shirt, grey pants hoisted aloft with a neck-tie knotted at the waist. Sandals, no socks. Scrawny neck, bruised sunken eyes behind thick charity shop bins. Thinning grey flat-top. I wonder if he's talked to anyone about Gwendoline's death.

When I move slightly, trying to get comfortable where I've parked myself on the sofa, the whole thing slips and slides like San Antonio platelets.

'Careful with that,' he warns, fumbling with the gas ring. 'It's only made out of books.'

What the? When I lift the corner of the Indian bedspread covering the seat I see what he means. Stacks of books arranged in the shape of a sofa. One's protruding. I tug it out and thumb through the opening pages. *Towards a Socialist Analysis of the Post-Fordist Millennium* by Matthew Maloney. What's this? Dedicated to Gwendoline Rhodes?

'Remaindered copies,' he explains, spooning condensed milk into filthy pock-marked mugs.

Ugh, I can't drink this shit! He's perched on his typing chair balancing his mug of tea with a golden tin of Boars Head on his lap, rolling a matchstick thin cigarette.

'How's Maria?'

'She's convalescing or she would have come with me.' He's hunching his shoulders uncomfortably, fiddling with his lighter, as I explain about the hystie. Defying claims that in post-modern society it's impossible to change the subject, I change the subject. 'Y'mind me asking, what is this place? It doesn't seem like an ordinary B & B.'

He smiles sardonically, blowing elegant smoke rings into the fug. 'It's a hostel for unmarried mothers.' Is he joking me?

'So what are you doing here?'

'I live here. I was rendered homeless and unemployable by Gwendoline and her gang at the council. They put me here to humiliate me. But I don't care where I live. They can't shut me up. So long as I have breath left in my body I will carry on my work. Exposing corruption. Some aspects of my life may be controlled from the town hall but they can't lock up my mind. It's the women who have to live here who've been inconvenienced.'

He regrets that his presence here makes life awkward for the mothers and mothers-to-be and takes pains to tell me.

'I always replace the lavatory seat after use. And I always use the bathroom after everyone else has finished. I don't enjoy trying to be invisible at all times. But invisibilisation is all part of the softening-up process. I'm being softened up for the kill.'

Man's dying to tell his paranoid tale. 'This is my prison cell,' he continues. 'As you see, we carry on, documenting the events of the last twenty-five years, identifying class traitors and exposing their dirty tricks. We retain our optimism in spite of the uphill task. Despair is the enemy of progress!'

When I ask him who's 'we', he smiles a secret little smile. 'At the moment we are very few,' he says softly.

I've spent hours and hours arguing with my mother

about exposure politics. What's left to expose? Everything's already out in the public domain and nobody gives a fuck. It's no longer possible that the masses don't know what's going on, that all the gullible creatures need is a few enlightened comrades to come along and explain the system for them and they'll rise-like-lions-after-slumber-in-unvanquishable-number.

The comrades were the gullible fools. Now there's nothing left to expose. Everything's hanging out in the most blatant way imaginable. Human beings get used to anything. Shit-eating becomes the norm. We're having our noses rubbed in it every day. Nothing left but the naked truth. The overclass has achieved a state in which there's no longer any point in lying. Now they've got everything they want they can even pretend to be honest and open – make a virtue out of it. Say they're sorry; say their prayers. End of story!

Today, however, I'm here to find out about Gwendoline's past, not to argue the toss with Matthew.

'Maria suggested I should come and talk to you about Gwendoline Rhodes.'

He asks me if I'm a journalist. When I say I'm not I swear he looks disappointed. But he's satisfied when I say Maria sent me to him to find out about Gwendoline, help innocent people who are being put in the frame for her murder, help prevent a miscarriage of justice.

'My mother suggested you knew her better than anybody.'

A nascent sense of shame alarms me. I don't want him to guess what I really do for a living. Dissembling's not an option with Matthew. He knows the council set-up better than anyone. I'm relying on his obsession with his own concerns to render him uninterested in my line of work.

'When did you last see Gwendoline?' I ask.

'Many years ago. We were close comrades for a while.

Very close. She had the brains and drive to make a brilliant contribution to the struggle. But she went rotten. What more can I say?'

What about their personal involvement. Did they shack up together, or what? No, better hold back in case he clams up.

He continues with a bitter expression, 'Her defection was a devastating blow. A bereavement. As far as I'm concerned the woman I knew died back then, when she betrayed her comrades to satisfy her vaulting ambition.'

'Erum, I notice you dedicated your book to her.'

'Ah well. We all have something regrettable in our past. An error of judgement. You see, the woman I thought I knew was a figment of my own wishful thinking. It was nobody's fault.'

The cigarette's dead on his lip but he keeps trying to get a draw out of it. 'Many of the old comrades from that time were far more corrupt than Gwendoline. For example, Orson Bainbridge and his clique were up to their necks, although he was never actually caught with his finger in the till. The nearest he came to disaster was the, ummer, affair with your mother.'

'Affair?'

'Oh, am I being terribly indiscreet? I understood that he betrayed her and then accused her of stalking him. Whatever the truth of that may be, it was Maria who forced him to retreat for a few years. That was the one and only time Orson had to walk the plank. Unfortunately, people have very short memories. He was able to worm his way back in after a while. The secret of Orson's success has always been to maintain his contacts, high and low, and get them into key posts where they come in useful at a later date.

'Orson would move from borough to borough. Finance Director here, Director of Housing there, aiming to end up as Chief Executive. He hasn't made it yet, as far as I know.'

He laughs his sardonic laugh again. 'But I was more personally affected by Gwendoline's betrayal. Purely on a political level, of course. We'd been called the Luxemburg and Liebknecht of our generation. 'Needless to say,' he smiles modestly, 'that was ridiculous. There was no mass movement to justify such an extravagant comparison. But that was typical of the movement in this country. No modesty. All the same, there was a feeling. You wouldn't understand unless you were there. As A.J.P. Taylor said of the revolutions of 1848, it was a moment when "history reached its turning point and failed to turn".'

The sky through the small window has clouded over, plunging us into ever deeper gloom. He relights his cigarette, repeatedly clicking an old Zippo, illuminating his mad-scientist face. Of course, I've heard it all before. 'Socialism has been completely repudiated . . . blah, blah.'

I recognise this language and I know how to please.

'Yeah. Bourgeois democracy is just as if two management teams are competing with each other to run the system.' And he's a tickled pinko.

At random I pluck a pamphlet from the stack beside me and start to read. Hey, this is more like it!

'A new era of world history has opened. From Prague to Peking a new world order has come into being which has freed itself from the orbit of imperialism. One third of humanity, under the leadership of communism, are building their countries anew, free from the domination of the exploiters and imperialism.

'British imperialism is in extreme decay. But it is not yet finished. It is striving to adopt many new forms and techniques to meet new conditions. Witness of this is written from Greece to Malaya, from the Gold Coast to Transjordan, and from Strachey's ground nuts to Cripps' Budget.'

What the fuck are Stratchey's ground nuts?

Speaking of extreme decay, a big dried leaf is stuck between two issues of *London Briefing*. When I pick it up by the stem and hold it to the light between thumb and forefinger – it's not a leaf – it's the flattened, dehydrated body of a dead mouse.

'Can I keep it?'

Without commenting on my discovery he takes a piece of typing paper and cleverly folds it into quarters to make an envelope.

'Put it in this.'

'You think Gwendoline killed herself?'

Matthew sticks out his bottom lip and shakes his head.

'Not the Gwendoline I knew. She was a fighter. Of course, you have to bear in mind, she may have changed utterly. But that was one aspect I can't imagine changing. Her tenacity.'

'Did you know she had a son?'

Matthew freezes. Cornered in his lair, haunted eyes, anguish and fear on his face. I'm wide-eyed at this snapshot of an endangered species, more than that – the last of an extinct species, a dodo.

'No. I didn't know.'

Then the shutter closes. His face resumes its sardonic expression. He and Gwendoline had parted company on acrimonious terms. Then he heard she'd taken a job with a glitzy management consultancy. That was his first indication that she'd actually gone over to the other side and it was a nasty shock. In those days, that sort of betrayal caused quite a stir. It was during the final stages of the mopping up exercise against the Left in the Labour Party.

'That was when they screwed me,' he says.

According to Matthew, him and Gwendoline were a team. He supplied creative accounting skills and Gwendoline had the political nous. They constructed an alternative council leadership on the Labour back benches. The Tories just used to sit in the gallery to watch the debates. Matthew and Gwendoline dominated the show, using every trick in the book to beat government cuts: leasing parking metres, juggling spending between financial years, capitalising housing repairs, spreading costs over sixty years, deferred purchase agreements. Gimmicks to avoid the real fight.

'We should have resigned immediately. Refused to administer the Tories' medicine right from the start. But we went along with the so-called dented shield policy to soften the effect of the cuts. Protect the public from the Tories.'

Gwendoline was one of the staunchest supporters of the dented shield, kidded herself that with his accounting genius and her looks they could beat the Tories at their own game.

'For a while we were on a roll. Increasing spending. We copied ideas from the Italian Communist Party, holding free festivals and so forth, taking on more staff, everyone was optimistic.'

When the game itself became more important than the politics, Matthew found himself pressured into sharp practice. No one could remember any more which policies had been initiated by the Tories and which by Labour. Behind the scenes, behind his back, Gwendoline was making secret deals with City bankers. Matthew resisted. She threw him to the wolves. Tabloid smears started appearing. Before long he was 'Mister Clause-Four-in-a-bed'.

'I was supposed to have slept with schoolgirls, been to S&M orgies, organised paedophile rings, eaten babies, the lot.'

The night the old party leader, the Welsh windbag, resigned was the end of the dented shield. After that councillors were falling over themselves to set up private companies. One scandal broke after another: council funding for privately owned children's homes where kids were being abused; Scientologists running old people's homes with council funding; school meals and street-cleaning contracts being dished out to the lowest bidder regardless of quality or past bankruptcy, to mention a few.

Our Gwendoline quietly moved across to a less controversial borough or had a spell as a consultant. There were rumours she was angling for a parliamentary seat. When this failed to materialise she re-emerged in her renewed, heightened guise as the Dragon Lady, employing her famous scorched earth policy to get rid of opposition, abandoning the cabinet system in favour of a hand-picked bunch of cronies. Those who were not part of her inner circle, which was constantly changing, were excluded from decision-making.

Matthew was finished. His reputation was so fucked he couldn't get a job as a maggot in a meat loaf. Instead of complaining about the serious damage to his job prospects he starts rambling on about how it all reminded him of the united front against fascism during the war, as expounded by Dimitrov, 'Which would you rather? Bourgeois democracy or fascism?'

The Gospel according to Matthew is that after the war, once the crisis had passed, the working class forgot their autonomy. They were stuck with the bourgies forever, melded together in one amorphous lumpen mush. His eyes have glazed over and it's going to be tough to drag him back to the present.

'Do you think Gwendoline was personally corrupt? I mean, was she on the take herself?'

'No. Definitely not. She was too ambitious to be interested in mere money. She wanted to run the country. Her ambition was huge. I have never known anybody as power-hungry. In the early years, I admired her energy.

Naively, I thought she genuinely believed in the politics we subscribed to. I was wrong. She merely used us as a stepping stone to high office. But she was not corrupt in terms of personal financial gain. No, definitely not.'

Yes, it must have stung. Labour's huge majority let in several of her former underlings from local government. One new MP had been a typist at housing when Gwendoline was on her ascent to the top of the department. Even Lib-Dems have been given Cabinet posts!

'One last thing,' I ask on impulse. 'Have you heard of a guy called Stan, an engineer? Hates pushy women with big shoulder pads?'

Matthew remembers that Stan was chief shop steward in the old set-up when he, Gwendoline and Orson were all working in the same borough. Orson had lost no time in recruiting Stan against Gwendoline.

'Stan had a pathological detestation of Gwendoline. What she stood for. Strong woman and all that. Not a pleasant character. What's he doing these days?'

'At present he's missing, but the police aren't bothered because he wasn't in the building when Gwendoline, er, died.'

He accompanies me to the bottom of the stairs. No sign of the AWOLs, though their fumes linger. And I leave Matthew freeze-framed in the doorway: a pathetic figure with his slightly bowed knees and ill-fitting specs.

eight

THE ENTRANCE TO THE squat had been an ambulance bay in the days when the building was used for its original purpose. When I bang my fist on the metal shutters, making a hell of a din, a peep-hole opens, a pink eye appears and the door slides up from the bottom. Big Hughie's on duty.

'Pat yourself all over,' he asks sheepishly. He's supposed to search for drugs since a new broom collective decided to ban certain mood-enhancing chemicals.

'Jesus, Hughie. It's great to be here. It's a nasty cruel world out there.' Now I've got his measure I'm easy with him. He's the sentimental type. I've learned how to have fun getting his chin to wobble.

'I don't know what would have become of my mother, if you hadn't taken her in hand, Hughie.' The dimple in his chin deepens and his eyes mist over.

'She's a great woman. I'm privileged to know her,' he says gruffly, as I finish patting myself down without revealing the tabbies cut into funky little shapes stashed inside my jacket.

Despite his soft side, Hughie's got the makings of an excellent bouncer. We've both been making the effort, getting to know each other better for Mum's sake. Even been for a drink a couple of times. One of those nights in the pub I witnessed hitherto unsuspected skills. A guy at the next table was taking the piss out of his drinking companion whose missus has just given birth to a baby girl. The guy's third daughter!

'You got poofter sperm!' the first man taunted.

'Who're you calling a fucking poof?'

Hughie didn't like the way their conversation was going. He hefted his bulk to their table and knocked their skulls together till their noses spurted blood and a couple of teeth plopped into their beers. Handy geezer to have around when brawn rather than brain is called for!

'Kitchen open, Hughie?'

'Naw. You know the rules, Montse. Glenys is doing the roster tonight. She's strict about eating after hours.'

I haven't met Glenys yet and I hate her already. 'Why do you let fuckers like that ponce off you?'

''Cause she's homeless, that's why.'

'She's a fucking camp commandant.'

Hughie comes out with the usual garbage. 'We gotta have discipline or the ruling class are gonna make mincemeat outta us.'

'Man, sounds like she *is* the ruling class!' No use arguing. From all accounts, Glenys is on a civilising mission and Hughie has fallen for it. This was a fun place to visit till Glenys arrived. She's got rid of all the New Age Travellers 'cause she caught them making acid in the bath. No wonder all the old skills are dying out! And now the whole place stinks of carbolic just like a real hospital. Glenys gets the inmates organised into cleaning squads, rubber boots, surgical masks, up and down the corridors scrubbing in unison. They stuffed up the holes where the rats got in and everyone takes turns on rat patrol. No one went for Mum's idea of bagging up a few juicy ones and letting them loose up in boogieville. If she wasn't laid up, Mum would do it herself.

When the NATs threw out a sack of flour which was full of weevils, Glenys went ape-shit. According to her, they should've got busy and picked all the weevils out. Waste not, want not.

Maria's still playing the wise matriarch, lying in bed with a gigantic spliff sticking out of her mouth, surrounded by yoof! She's telling them about a protest she cooked up against the National Fraud Hotline when it first began. 'Operation No-Grass: Nothing Organised: Grass Roots Against Sneaks and Snoops'.

'Are you amongst the millions of right-thinking citizens disgusted and angered by the actions of a tightly organised gang of fraudsters? If you want to report a case of cheating and deception, report whichever of the unnumberable instances of theft you feel particularly incensed by.

'The loss of rights, incomes, jobs, housing, training, care, equality and democracy stolen from us by those in power. For example, removing benefits from the unemployed, taking older people's homes to pay for care, privatisations, fat cats creaming off vast profits, devastating cuts to public services, destruction of NHS, We wuz robbed!'

Every Friday Maria and her cronies, whoever she could rope in, would ring 0800 854 440. Once the operator said, 'Thank you for calling the National Fraud Hotline,' they'd start,

'A gang of crooks is ripping off the public.'

'What's the address?'

'They operate from a large building overlooking the river.'

At the time I was on the receiving end of a lot of flack

from Maria over my job. For some reason she seemed to think there was a link between me and the hotline whereas we're a different department altogether. Well, I happen to know a couple of the people who operate those phonelines and they're very highly trained. I don't believe they'd have let my mother and her mates go on like she claimed.

'Oh, that's not a problem,' Mum said. 'You can keep them talking for a long time before they get it. The kind of people who do jobs like that are totally thick. They're the dregs.'

My cheeks were stinging with anger. Looking back, I don't know why I got so worked up. I should have treated her like a naughty kid because that's her problem. She's never grown up. But a few weeks later, she got her comeuppance and even though I was sickened by the whole affair, deep down I felt a dull ache of pleasure.

What happened was, thinking she'd use irony to shock, Maria told the operator,

'My neighbour's hiding a Jew in the attic.'

'What's the name of this person?'

'Who?'

'Not the Jew. The person who's hiding the Jew in their attic.'

'I'm not sure if I should tell you.'

'Whatever you say will be treated with the utmost confidence. Is that what's worrying you?'

'Yes.'

'Just tell me if it's a man or a woman? Not the Jew. I mean the person who's hiding the Jew.'

'A woman.'

'There's no need to worry about anyone finding out it was you who rang us. We can't even trace this call. I've got a form in front of me that we have to fill in and we don't even write down whether it was a man or woman who phoned in with the information. No one can possibly find out it was you. What is the woman's name?'

My mother kept silent and the operator kept shouting and cajoling, 'Don't hang up!' But Maria felt sick, dropped the phone and staggered out of the phone box in shock.

When she sees me come into the room she has the sense to cut her recitation short and soon asks them all to leave so she can hear my report on Matthew. First I show her the mouse skeleton. She wants it for a dream catcher to hang over her bed. Then I have to describe every inch of the place where he lives, recount every word that he uttered and go over it again and again until she's satisfied nothing's been left out. Of course, I've deliberately left something out. I can't bring myself to tell her what Matthew said about her having a fling with Orson. My mother's sexuality disgusts me. I don't care what people do in the privacy of their own homes, so long as they don't ram it down our throats!

'So, he thinks the police are on the wrong track? She wouldn't top herself? Did he say anything about Tunbridge?'

'He reckons, if anything crooked's going on, Tunbridge is in it up to his eyeballs.'

'Did he say anything about me?'

'Not as such. But he did say, "I remember your mother. She's a good woman."'

Maria's chuffed but feigns otherwise. 'Good woman? What's he blathering about? He'll ruin my reputation, going round saying things like that.'

'Hey, Mum. What are Strachey's ground nuts?'

She bellows with laughter. 'Got an hour to spare?'

Unwittingly, I've unleashed one of her favourite hobby horses, 'the parasitic economy of the British Empire'.

In 1947 – the Labour Government grabbed three million acres of land in Tanganyika and handed over £25 million to Unilever to develop vast ground nut plantations. John Strachey, who was Minister of Food at the time, got it in the nuts when the scheme flopped.

'Mum! How'd you get the puff in here?'

'Glenys says it's OK for pain relief.'

Bloody Glenys again. The woman's definitely riding for a fall when I meet her.

Weezie's packing her stuff.

'What's going on?'

'I'm tired of your fantasising, Montse. It's doing my head in. I'm moving back to Widdecombe. You knew this arrangement was only temporary. I can't stand it any more. Not knowing what's going on. The police have been here today. I opened the door and they just marched in. I'm sorry, but I couldn't stop them.'

'Calm down. We can sort this out. What police? Uniformed?'

'Grey suits.'

Weezie's wrappin Puja in his sling and tying him on to her back. She picks up her bags and makes for the door.

'Thanks for your hospitality, Montse. I know you mean well, but I can't live like this.'

I let them go without a word, grab a six-pack from the fridge and plunge on to my sofa clinging to the remote. I didn't mean things to end this way. I was putting a few feelers out at work, trying to find a void for Weezie to move into. If only she'd waited.

Peking, Afghanistan, Palestine, then Birmingham, Brighton and London shimmer across the screen. I watch in a disturbed stupor till, bingo! – familiar faces in my face. A clip they've shown repeatedly since Gwendoline's death of her running the gauntlet of a demo outside the town hall. Wheelchair users pinning her beside her car. One man's trying to shackle himself to her bumper. She grabs him by the shoulders and sends his chair flying. Cries of 'Sieg Heil!'.

Before I can figure out what's going on one of the council cleaners I disturbed in Gwendoline's office – or should I say, disturbed me? – pops up on the screen telling a reporter how she'd been amazed to discover that the woman she'd taken for Gwendoline was, in fact, an imposter! I nearly fall off my sofa again. The police request this imposter to come forward to eliminate herself from their inquiries. All I fucking need! I hope my bloody mother isn't watching. Get a grip. Don't panic. Do the slow breathing. There's no reason anyone would connect the cleaner's vague description with me. From now on I'll have to keep myself well out of the way of that cleaner, maybe take time off. I've just been on compassionate leave but I'm still owed a week's TOIL.

Couple of hours later I'm working my way through the last of the Red Stripe when the doorbell throws me into another panic. Weezie's come back! Standing on the mat, damp and dejected.

'Where've you been?'

'God, Montse. You're trolleyed.'

'Am not. Even if I was, it's a free fucking country. I can lie on my own sofa in my own fucking flat and get drunk as a skunk if I wanna.'

Her hair's in rats tails and there's a bead of water trembling off the tip of her nose. Puja's completely covered in wrap-round shawls and scarves. Weezie stomps in and starts unbundling.

'They've given my room to someone else,' she sniffs, shaking herself like a dog. 'That horrible woman, Sally, says you told her I wouldn't be back. Now the council will say I've made myself intentionally homeless. We've got nowhere to go now, thanks to you. We'll have to stay here tonight.'

When Weezie goes all self-righteous and whiny, I go right off her. Only the other night I say something quite inoffensive about Englishness and she goes into one, prating on about a 'gentler tradition' — something akin to Eastern mysticism. Land of Hope and Glory? Cheeky chappies dancing round a maypole with Lucinda Lambton?

'Don't worry, Louise. I'll see you right. I never let you down yet. Have I? Have I?' But she goes into the bedroom — my fucking bedroom — and, without saying jack shit, closes the door. My heart contracts.

On principle, I refuse to pay out till the insurance comes through. My car's still in the same shitty condition as it was when I picked it up. But the engine runs OK.

Today's Saturday and I'm meeting Billy at his grandmother's house in the country. With a road map laid out on the dashboard, more by luck than design, I've negotiated myself to the address he gave me. Out front there's an overgrown garden with a broken gate; at the back, a field containing a collection of rusting farm implements. A festoon of cobwebs drape from the door frame as I ply a grotesque gargoyle knocker. Ratta tat tat.

A real mumsy opens the door. A careworn mouse in a frilly apron. Gwendoline must have got her out of a Bisto advertisement.

'Mrs Rhodes?'

'No,' she says. 'But I am the mother of Gwendoline Rhodes.'

'Billy in?'

She's hesitant but the gap's widening. When I hold up my ID with the official looking badge, the door opens. 'Come in please. I apologise for the state of the house,' she says. Through a dark hall there's a cheerful country kitchen, armchairs bursting with horsehair, big table and aga saga cooker. At a glance I can tell she's the simple type. Not what I expected. And I don't mean simple badly. Think uncomplicated, unsophisticated. Not like her scheming, power-hungry bitch of a daughter.

'I'll put the kettle on,' she says.

Sitting at the rough wooden table, I'm composing my face the way they do in cop shows when breaking bad news. Except, in this instance, the news has already been broken, maybe by my friend, for I do think of him now as such, DC Chiang.

She lifts one corner of her pinny and dabs her eyes. 'I always knew this would happen one day. The knock at the door in the middle of the night.'

Gwendoline's timepiece makes it half past three in the afternoon. Obviously the old girl's confused. Perhaps she's watched too many old gangster movies on TV. A knock in the middle of the night, Cagney's brother goes to the door. Upstairs, their dear old mum changes the bedding in readiness for Jimmy's homecoming. The brother opens the door. Cagney falls into the room, nailed to a plank, dead as a doornail. And there's one where he's on top of this giant leggo and it's about to blow. 'Top of the world, ma, top of the world!' It all goes up in flames. You forgive Cagney anything because he loves his old mother.

Gwendoline's mother won't sit down. She fusses around making tea, rattling biscuit tins. 'She lived too hard for a woman. She lived too fast. I tried to warn her, but she was just like her father. There was no telling her.'

'Do you think it's possible she could have taken her own life?'

'Never, never never. She came from noble stock on her father's side. Strong people. Strong personalities. Not the type. Only to avoid capture by the enemy. Then suicide might be the honourable thing. Not to be taken alive. But Gwendoline had the world to conquer and of course she had no enemies.

'As a mother, I feel in my bones she wasn't ready to die. If anyone was to blame it must have been me. There must have been something I should have done that I did not do, something that a mother should know instinctively. P'raps something I forgot.'

Is there really a maternal and preternatural hot line to an offspring's motivations?

We both jump when the door bursts open and Billy irrupts into the kitchen. First he doesn't know me. Just stands there looking blank.

'Oh Billy,' his grandmother cries, as if it's a tea party, 'isn't it nice? You've got a friend come to visit.'

His failure to instantly recognise me is a worry. All I want out of life is a bit of sanity. How comes everyone's nuts except me? He's shaking slightly and goes into baby mode, his granny fussing over him. A nice cuppa will set him up. That's all she knows. The boy's crying out for something stronger. He jerks the mug, spilling his tea and she lovingly mops up the puddles.

'The cops say its OK to go ahead with the funeral,' he mumbles, jiggling his feet. 'Mr Bainbridge is gonna help me to do whatever.'

'Bainbridge is a crook!' Why can't I keep my big fat gob shut? Billy's immediately suspicious. His hands are shaking so bad he's having trouble getting a skin out of a packet of Rizlas. So I help him, taking some of the mixture he's got stored in a suede pouch round his neck.

'Not another control freak,' he says, referring to me. When I finish rolling up he pokes out his cat-like tongue so I can moisten the Rizla. Man, I must be going soft in my old age!

'I've got nothing to gain,' I say, trying to deflect his resentment, 'I'm just giving you a bit of advice.'

'We won't get the money, Evelyn,' he wails.

Her head wobbles slightly, 'We've always managed, Billy. Just the two of us.' He giggles, out of control, voice high-pitched. She looks at him pityingly and tells me with a tinge of bitterness, 'Billy hasn't got the character his grandfather had, or that Gwendoline had for that matter. You'd never catch either of them crying or tittering like a silly tart.'

Suddenly he's angry. 'Don't you understand, you silly old cow,' he shouts. 'If they think it's suicide, we don't get the fucking money!'

She carries on talking as if he's not there. 'Billy's worried that Gwendoline's insurance policies will be invalidated if her employers succeed in having her death registered as a suicide. He doesn't seem to appreciate that everyone must make their own way in life. We can't always rely on the state or hope for unexpected windfalls.'

Abruptly Billy gets up from the table. I get the strong feeling that hatred is propelling him from her presence. I follow. 'Hey, Billy. You called me. Remember? What's going on?'

His room smells of musk and old cheese, the room of a boy, and yet Billy's age could be anywhere between sixteen and thirty-six. The walls are painted black, model aeroplanes lurch from the ceiling, his bed – a mattress on the floor – is bedraggled, his floor strewn with soiled underpants and socks. He flings himself on the bed and I get down on my haunches resting my back against a wonky chest of drawers.

'Fucking Gwendoline done me out of my inheritance,' he whines, between drags. What inheritance? Is he talking about the money Gwendoline worked her bollocks off to earn, or some other money that I don't know about? Funny how in tune I feel with Gwendoline now she's dead. Sure, she was a hard bitch, but she worked for what she got, she didn't lie round all day wanking herself off, waited on hand and foot by her granny. I'm the one who should be upset. Had Gwendoline lived, my career would have taken off like a rocket. She saw my worth. She knew guts when she saw them.

The puff's settling Billy, not that it stops him talking. Over and over, I hear the story of how he was brought up by his granny, was in denial about her not being his mother, even though the birth dates didn't add up. Nothing was said by anyone in the family about their unorthodox arrangement. Gwendoline was like an older sister. A selfish bitch *par excellence*.

As Billy talks I begin to understand that I'm in no way a special confidante. He'd confide in anyone. Anyone ready to listen. Even Orson. Now I can see clearly that he would talk in exactly the same way to Orson Bainbridge, holding nothing back. Gwendoline's family set-up will be an open book to Orson.

Driving back from Billy's, mulling over the various problems I've got on my plate, my mind returns to my own domestic scene. My relationship with Weezie has gone from warm to tepid to gelid in the space of a couple of weeks. Simultaneously, I feel closer and closer to Puja. I'd do anything to get his approval. The front room's chocka with expensive toys and the most absorbent, exorbitantly priced nappies. The more I give, the colder Weezie grows. And her stubborn refusal to accept that Widdecombe Hall is no place for a baby makes it impossible to get back to where we were when she first moved in with me. But I've got a brilliant idea. The ideal place for Weezie and Puja is the squat: my mother, Weezie and Puja all under one roof where I can easily keep tabs on them all.

Even though I haven't yet changed direction; still bowling along the same dreary dual carriageway, flashing past the gated estates of the super-rich bastards who head up the City challenges, enterprise executives and all the other non-governmental instruments of government of the people, above the people and screw the people; I know I'm now heading for the squat. This feels like some kind of solution. A place of safety for Weezie and Puja. Weezie could be a mediating influence between me and my mother. She might be able to get Maria to understand me a bit better. The squat would be a secure place which is socially acceptable to Weezie with her communal tendencies. Maria, I think, would like Puja. She usually likes babies. Except, of course, her own.

I get on the mobile. 'Louise? Hey, guess where I'm phoning from. The countryside! Hang on a minute. I've got some jerk right up my tail.'

I'm putting my foot down and I'm not losing him. He's filling my rear-view mirror. Thick, meaty face. Not a face I know.

'Weezie? You still there? Lock the front door and don't let anyone in. You hear me? I can't explain now. I've gotta shut up and drive.'

Now she'll really be pissed.

Whoever the geezer behind me is, he's a sloppy operator. All he knows is to sit in the car with his foot flat down on the floor. Doesn't know how to coax a car. Really drive it. Thinks he's cool, pressing up against my bumper.

But I'm releasing the gas pedal slowly, little by little, and I'm pressing on the clutch. Now I'm coasting. Stupid arsehole's pushing me along. The needle's falling. I'm going down through the gears. He's giving me the two fingers. I grab a hefty map book and post it through the sunshine roof. The wind whips it over the car and on to his bonnet and it's flapping against his windscreen. Now I'm down to third and he's still in fifth, so I burn rubber and we part company.

In the distance I see him hauling his wheel and careening into the central reservation. A plume of black smoke billows up and the driver's out of the car, a bouncing dot on the horizon.

The squat's the safest place for Weezie and Puja. Safe as Fort Knox. Padlocks, double locks, chains, boards, the lot. Crossing the road after parking my car, still a couple of hundred yards to walk, and I get a feeling as if something nasty's crawling down the back of my neck. Fornications under the skin.

With a great whoosh of air a car appears out of nowhere, driving straight at me. I have to fling myself out of its path and it goes by like a blur, with a hint of mustard about the man at the wheel. He could have been Stan. Put it down to feeling shaky from the experience on the motorway, but I start yelling and running as hard as I can towards the metal shutters outside the squat.

Hughie's heard the commotion. He's got the shutters up and I'm in. 'Anything you want sorted, Montse?' I'm shaking but I manage to reply, 'Nah, just some nutter who needs to learn to drive.'

Mum's complaining of wind, holding her stomach and making horrible faces. 'Anyone got any linseeds?' I ask immediately. Of course, they have. Every conceivable kind of seed, grain and pulse is stored in their kitchen. I boil up a handful of linseeds in a disgusting chipped pan and Mum swallows the resulting grey glup as best she can. Relief follows within half an hour. My approval ratings rise a few degrees although Mum can't resist making some crack about my cooking. I tell them my mate and her little baby need a place to stay. They agree to put it to the next meeting of the whole squat, two nights away. It's OK for me to attend the meeting and bring Weezie and Puja along.

When the others drift off to attend a strategy meeting organised by Glenys, I get a rare chance to speak to my mother on her own.

'Mum, do you know if Orson Bainbridge has ever been involved in anything violent?'

'No, he's too clever for that. He's like Gwendoline. He pays his lackeys to do his dirty work for him.' Lackeys! How many times has she used that word about me? Again I've allowed myself to be humiliated. When am I going to live down my affiliation with Gwendoline? If only Mum had known Gwendoline like I did, she'd understand that things are never that simple. Ask anyone and we'll all say we want a better world. Gwendoline's way was different. She'd only just laid her hands on the levers of power when she was cut off in her prime, before she could even get started.

But Mum was saying, 'I'd love to get inside the head of a person like that. Didn't you tell me she was seeing a shrink? I wouldn't mind being a fly on the wall when she was having her head read.'

My heart stops when I see Chiang's car's parked outside my flat with the DC sitting inside it. Something's happened to

Weezie and Puja. But he grins and rolls his window down when I rush over.

'Sorry to be a pest, Ms Letkin. Can we talk?'

Anything that delays fronting up to Weezie.

'Yeah, but not inside. My flatmate's already pissed about your previous unwelcome visits.' He opens the passenger door and I get in. 'Unwelcome visits?' he repeats, with a puzzled expression. 'I've only spoken to your friend on the telephone. Never visited before.'

'Don't wind me up. The place was trashed,' I tell him.

'Not by me or my colleagues,' he says.

We end up at the Standard in Lisle Street and I'm grateful to my citizen-of-the-world mother for educating me in the use of chopsticks.

I keep waiting for him to quiz me about my relationship with Gwendoline and my mind's racing with things to say. But he's not asking about Gwendoline, he's asking about me. Do I have any brothers and sisters? Are my parents alive and well? We've consumed a couple of Tiger beers and I can feel my tongue loosening dangerously. How did I get into my line of work? He laughs when I tell him about the Job Club. But looks sympathetic when I explain how my mother doesn't approve.

'Some members of my family are not very keen on my line of work, either,' he admits, ordering another Tiger.

Feeling I'm giving too much away, I seize the opportunity to steer the conversation in a different direction. His family. He's happy to talk. His parents left mainland China after the revolution. His mother remembers hiding in a cellar as the Red Army marched into Beijing. His grandmother, now trying to get out of Hong Kong, still makes jokes along the lines that when Mao Tsetung farted the whole world stank. DC Chiang has got relatives all over. San Francisco, Hong Kong, Canada. He's a real citizen of the world. He looks aghast when I tell him how my mother supported the Cultural Revolution and taught me to read using as my primers, 'The Foolish Old Man Who Moved Mountains' and 'The Cock Crowed at Midnight'.

'You know, Montse,' he frowns, leaning across the table, 'Children were encouraged to inform on their own parents.'

'God,' I say, 'that stinks.' We laugh.

The restaurant's thinning out. We're among a handful of patrons still eating. 'I believe I can trust you, Montse. This is highly confidential but I thought I should tell you what's happening with the Rhodes case. The powers that be have made up their minds her death was the result of suicide. There's a strong possibility the murder investigation will be wound up and the papers handed over to the Fraud Squad. A lot of money's gone missing. Between ourselves, I don't agree it was suicide. It doesn't feel right. Why would an ambitious career politician become involved in a fraud of this nature? What do you think? You worked closely with Gwendoline Rhodes. What's your gut feeling?'

That's how it comes about that I end up telling him the lot: Matthew, Orson, Billy, Granny; sitting in the Standard at two in the morning with a knot of disgruntled waiters huddled down one end of the room and DC Chiang ordering up Tiger beers like there's no tomorrow. The only piece of information I withhold is about the Rolex which I've more or less decided to keep.

My finest moment is when he says,

'By the way, I want you to know I believe you about the tape. Why would you invent such a thing?'

The last thing I remember is him asking,

'Do you know anything about her trips to the Channel Islands?'

'Channel Islands?' I say, trying hard. 'No, not the Channel Islands. But I heard something about the Scillies.'

nine

I'M ENJOYING AN UNUSUALLY peaceful state of mind, considering it's morning and I'm not a morning person. Weezie and Puja are flaked out in front of Teletubbies and I'm relieved that I can creep out of the flat without a confrontation. As I go I'm grabbing a letter from the mat and ripping it open on my way to the car with rain pissing on my head. The insurers are paying up. Maybe things are going to get better.

On her return from visiting Widdecombe Hall, Weezie had said nothing to indicate that Sally, the warden, had blown my cover, but a loose cannon like that needs checking out. If I don't keep a check on the situation, things get out of control and I hate people acting out stuff behind my back, so I drive over there on my way to work. South of the borough a new rail terminus is being built, gateway to Europe, on the spot where I once sprawled on the grass with my mates, bunking off school for a sociable puff, watching the world go by. All concreted over, malled in and made private.

Skips are out front at Widdecombe, filling with broken beds, soiled blankets, battered suitcases, umbrellas, scruffy bits of clothing and shoes, broken specs, even a nicotine-stained pair of gnashers. Scaffolding's going up. The pigeons are back in the roof, unaware that the building's being gutted beneath them. Workmen are hammering a developer's board to a stake. You've got to hand it to the council. They can move fast when they want to. The efficient speed with which the place has been cleared takes my breath away.

No Sally? And what happened to all the poor bastards who lived here? After driving round the block a couple of times, peering through the pissing rain, I'm coming to the conclusion it's no bad thing. The place was a dump. The occupants will be better off somewhere else. Now Weezie will have no choice but to move to the squat.

So I'm mellow when I reach the office. Occasionally, I can get this feeling of imminent doom, as if a huge pile of shit's going to drop down on my head any minute. Nothing happens. Other times when I'm experiencing a deep sense of spiritual well-being, feeling inalienable and exempt from life's travails; *voilà*, the shit descends.

Roger rises puffily from his desk when I breeze in. The late, great Gwendoline is credited with saying of him, 'He can brighten a room just by leaving it.' And, 'Roger's such a clubbable chap. Quick somebody, hand me a club!' With Gwendoline's witticisms in mind, I'm probably smirking a little. Perhaps that's why he's looking at me with more than day-to-day hatred.

His hairy, pork chop mitts are stirring a pile of papers. 'I've been going over your record. Your figures are deceptively high, concealing relatively low levels of net satisfaction. Actual revenues generated by the type of offender you are apprehending are low. So, from where I'm sitting, Ms Letkin, you are far from efficient. You see, it's my job to look after the budget of this department to ensure value for money. One of the cases I found in your file was brought against one of our own bailiffs!'

'Come off it, Roger, he was a council tax evader. He

was registered at a phoney address, claiming dole in four different boroughs. Are you saying it's one rule for us and another one for them?'

Roger scowls. 'OK, Letkin, we'll let that one lie for now. How do you account for your ridiculous allegation against Julian Pike?'

Acting the drama queen, he slaps his forehead and falls back in his chair, shaking his head in false amazement, pursing his mouth into a tight little wedding ring, 'Do you honestly believe that a Minister of the Crown would sleep with a slag from one of the worst estates in the borough?'

'What are you saying, Roger? Are you saying our estates are not fit for a Cabinet Minister to fuck in? I was only going by the book. She names the father, I'm duty bound to hand the case over to Child Support.'

'There are more serious matters which have to be taken into consideration,' Roger goes on. 'Ms Letkin, it grieves me deeply to have to tell you that you are recommended for deletion pending a full investigation. You will be given the opportunity to answer for your actions at an internal tribunal.'

'Deletion? What for?'

'For bringing this department into disrepute. Go home, Letkin, and wait to hear from us.'

Start the day the Letkin way. Suspended. For what?

Now Weezie's gone po-face on me. Refuses to spend another night under my roof. Dumps her stuff in the car as if a bag of baby clothes is weighty as a sack of rice. Puja's in good spirits though, blowing bubbles and gurning sweetly through the folds of his mother's voluminous garments.

Hughie won't look at me as he pats us down for drugs.

'I know it's slack, not waiting for the meeting, but I'm throwing myself on your mercy. Louise ain't got nowhere to go. Contractors are knocking down the mother and baby home as we speak and she can't go back to the council.'

'I dunno,' Hughie says. 'It's not for me to say. The decision's up to the collective.'

The place is uninviting. Grim, grey concrete. Cold comfort in Hughie's expression. Not how I'd imagined Weezie and Puja's joyful arrival at the squat with everyone making a fuss of the baby and marvelling at Weezie's useful domestic skills.

Bolstered with fat cushions, Mum's reclining on her mattress like Lady Muck, reading out her horoscope.

'"Someone you think is your friend is doing you down and someone you think is doing you down is really your friend." God, that's typical,' she shouts, flinging the paper into a far corner of the room. 'These things are designed to wind me up!'

Clocking us standing in the doorway she rolls her eyes as if to say 'here's trouble'.

Whenever she sees a baby she always makes the same quip at my expense, 'I'm still suffering from post-natal depression.' I'm bracing myself for it but she only groans and holds her belly.

'I could murder a cuppa', she says.

Ice rink sky. White cold sun. Perfect day for a funeral. Though watching as ever from the periphery, I feel I'm somehow central to the proceedings, connected and controlling while remaining remote out of my own choice; observing the crowd gathering at the crem. Orson, Roger, the mayor, a couple of nonentity MPs. Not a large gathering, but, in its own way, distinguished enough to draw a solitary news camera.

Like me, Matthew lurks on the verges. And there's my workmate, Maureen, her piercings coruscating in the harsh white light. As the hearse and official cars arrive, Orson is up front, schmoozing forward with the parson to receive the chief mourners, the dear departed's mother and son. Old Evelyn's dressed in forties finery, black feathers in her hat.

Matthew has an open view of Billy but doesn't see him. If he did, I wonder whether he'd register the resemblance. Two stick insects, made from the same material. One ancient, brittle. The other immature, flaccid. Thin cigarettes dangling from protruding lower lips. Nervy and jerky. Hollow cheeked and hollow chested. Am I the only one here who suspects a connection between them? Or does everyone know their secrets except them? Is that how it is with family secrets? Family are the last to know? Perhaps me and my mother are observed by strangers who know things about us. The existence and whereabouts of my father or my grandparents? Perhaps I've passed them in the street or sat next to them on the bus.

Among the mourners, only Maureen acknowledges me.

Dunno know what I'm waiting for. To while away the time I go for a wander in the garden of remembrance, reading one tombstone after another like a novel. One grave has a statuette of an angel with one arm broken off. The plinth is inscribed, 'Oh for the touch of a hand that is gone.' In a long out-house like a brick bus shelter I find hundreds of plaques with photographs of the departed set into the walls. No one I know.

Once the biz is done inside the chapel, Maureen comes to find me.

'Didn't see you inside,' she says.

'Didn't go in. Been looking round. Wanna laugh?'

I show her the angel with the arm missing. We sit on a stone slab, have a smoke and a laugh and I offer her a lift. 'Maybe come for a drink?'

'Gawd, it's boring at work without you,' she tells me in the pub. 'But you're better off out of it. You can always live on your wits.' Her beer glass keeps clicking against the rings in her lip. What would it be like to kiss a girl with pierced lips?

' 'ere, Monz, is it true you're having it away with Gwendoline's son?'

After a few jars kick in, plus the comfort of shooting the breeze with someone who bears me no grudge and whom I find absolutely neutral, that is, I don't hate her and I don't love her, I begin the ascent into recovery. I begin to believe I can bounce back. Ideas start coming thick and fast. If I want, I can stay out all night drinking, go back to my own fucking flat and fall down on the floor any time I like without having to account to anyone. I can piss in my pants if I want to. I can throw up down my own lavatory if I want to. And I can lie in bed all day tomorrow if I want to without having to look at Louise's sour puss.

'Hey, Maureen, wanna blast? Find out what really happened to Gwendoline?'

Collecting night soil would be easier than getting a reaction from Maureen. And yet she'd complained of boredom induced by the lack of my company. So there's hope.

A revelation has come to me that breaking into Gwendoline's therapy van would be a straightforward job for a pair of pros like me and Maureen. The vehicle, an Espace, may contain records of clients' sessions. I got my inspiration when I remembered how the Menendez brothers got caught. Their therapist broke the patient–client confidentiality.

The beauty of my plan is that Weezie, my mother and Hughie and probably even Glenys will be forced to give me the benefit of their respect when I pull off my brilliant coup. The balance of moral probity will tip in my favour. I'm not the petty snitch they take me for but the uncoverer of an important piece of intelligence which someone like my mother, who still believes in the magic of 'exposure politics', will want in the public arena. Thanks to little me, it fucking will be!

Shall I consult Chiang Chou? Yes, the DC has divulged his second name and has invited me to call him Joe. After all, as he says, he's just an ordinary Joe. Or is it wiser to wait until after the event, in case an unforeseen hitch occurs? Maureen is not the most reliable or desirable of assistants, though an ally, however modest, is a luxury to which I'm unaccustomed. Aggressive beggars can't be choosy.

'Well?'

'I'll do it if there's money in it,' she says.

I'm shocked! Not that she's asked to be paid, but shocked at the realisation that I, Montse Letkin, had expected her to jump at the chance to do something for me out of personal loyalty. And she didn't.

ten 10

TILL MY DISCIPLINARY I'M barred from entering the town bloody hall. So here I am, wanting to pee like a wild horse, waiting opposite for Maureen to come out. Who's to notice if I nip up the ladies for a quick slash?

I made the right decision. In the nick-a-time relief comes splurging. As I'm leaving the bathroom, a woman barges through the door, our bodies bouncing off each other angrily. Not wishing to draw attention to myself, I keep my lip zipped. But, fuck me, if the woman isn't only Karen, my bête noir, or, should I say, bête blanc.

'Montse Letkin, you're *banned* from this building,' she shrieks, leaving me no alternative but to reply in kind. Push comes to shove, nothing violent as such, but I ain't hanging round to argue the toss. Hurtling downstairs, I hit the ground floor running.

Outside, Maureen's stomping up and down on the slippery pavement, seriously yomping a mouthful of gum. Does she chew to concentrate, or does she concentrate to chew? I've come to stop her from going ahead with our mad plan. In the cold light of morning, breaking into the psycho-van doesn't seem so brilliant.

'What's happnin'?'

'Walk on fast, and listen to this! I go upstairs for a slash and guess who I bump into? Only that fucking Karen!'

'But, Montse, you're *banned!*'

'I had to pee. Bad!'

'You're bang out of order going in there. Her 'n Orson are tight as a sparrow's arse lately.'

'Think they're screwing?'

'Dunno, but I seen them going to lunch 'n that.'

A cop car draws up alongside us and I'm smiling idiotically, expecting ordinary Joe to be inside. Or, maybe he's sent a car to collect me? Take me for lunch or something? Uniform gets out.

'Montse Letkin?'

'That's me.'

Maureen legs it, leaving me with my faded grin.

'Come with us, Miss Letkin.'

'What for?'

'We need to eliminate you from certain inquiries which we are pursuing.'

Passersby eyeing me up and down like I'm a talking turd. Scurrying by. Not one of the bastards stepping up to ask 'Why are you harassing that woman!' What choice do I have but to get in the car? Maureen's face, a pale disc, recedes into the distance.

Billy's at the station, hunched in a booth with WPC Cattermole, knees drawn up, mouth working overtime: mother, grandmother, selfish bitch, tumbling out. Jerks his head as he sees me. Same blank eyes as in his grandmother's kitchen the other day.

'Can I see DC Chiang?'

My personal zoo keeper shakes his head. No point asking if I can make a phone call. Who's to call?

Orson's arrived, telling them he's come for Billy. His solicitor's attached to his elbow. The cops make him wait.

I'm marched into another booth. A cop I haven't seen before begins an interrogation. 'Are you Montse Letkin?'

'Am I charged with anything?'

'We're investigating a number of telephone calls which were made to the late Gwendoline Rhodes shortly before her death. At the moment we can't tell you more than that, we can only request you to help with our inquiries on a voluntary basis. Will you co-operate?'

He plunges on, taking my silence as a yes. 'Did you at any time make a telephone call in which you informed Gwendoline Rhodes that you had possession of a valuable item belonging to her?'

What if I did leave a couple of messages on her answering machine? Is that a crime? I wish I could remember exactly what I said. Orson must've found the tape and handed it over to the police. Or, has he simply listened to the tape and tipped them off anonymously, hoping to drop me in it? The detective is waiting for an answer.

Incarceration has a certain allure. Night in a bare cell. The clang of iron on iron. Alone in the dark, thinking of nothing at all. No one to get at me. Emerging heroically into the light. Describing my wrongful detention to crowds of supporters and reporters.

'I tried to contact Ms Rhodes shortly before she died to inform her that I had her watch.'

'Why didn't you give the watch to her son when you saw him on the evening of blahdy blah.' He quotes the time and date of the do at the Red Carnation. And some other dates which I don't recognise.

'I didn't have it then, did I?'

'Where is the watch now?'

'On my arm.'

I slide the watch on to the table in front of me. They

turn it this way and that, one of them puts it in a hanky and pretends to bash it with his shoe.

'Not the real thing, is it? Nice copy, mind. One of the best I've come across. Gives the illusion of prosperity, doesn't it, Ms Letkin. Boosts the old morale, no doubt. Nothing the matter with that. Spreading a bit of happiness. See, I'm a socialist *and* a policeman. We're all socialists now, aren't we, sergeant? Don't you think it's nice that the Labour Party have reclaimed the flag?'

'Lovely jubbly, sir.'

Whatever they're after, the watch is not it. The ugly bastard opposite dangles it off the end of his ball point and lets it drop on the desk in front of me. Quickly I shove it back up my arm.

'If you tell me what it is you're looking for, maybe I can help?'

They're not impressed by my kind offer.

'There's no maybes about it. If you know anything about Gwendoline's little racket you'd better say so now, for your own good.'

'I want to speak to DC Chiang.'

'Chiang? That sounds like one of them oriental names, doesn't it? We don't have any oriental gentlemen attached to this station, do we, sergeant?'

'Not that I know of, sir.'

Dittohead!

'Have you ever been to Guernsey, Miss Letkin? For any reason? On an errand for your boss, perhaps?'

'I've never been nowhere.'

Orson's in the lobby. No sign of the solicitor but he's got Billy in tow. 'Now isn't this a truly happy happenstance,' he exclaims. 'Two lovely young people in the poo and

Uncle Orson rides to the rescue. What are you doing here, Ms L?'

I'm saying nothing. If Orson handed the tape over to the police, he knows full well why they've called me in.

Billy's eyes are pinned out and he's snivelling into his hand.

'Buck up, old chap, you're free to go. You too, Miss L. Allow me give you both a lift. Wherever you're going.'

Whenever silly tarts in horror films go unaccompanied and unarmed into haunted, spooky houses, I'm always first to shout whadda-loada-crapola! Why would she go in there on her own? Stupid bitch! However, here am I – Billy doesn't count, he'd be worse than useless in a crisis – getting in a car with Orson. Even though this seems a bad idea, at least I'm doing it in a crowded street with my hand on the handle, ready to jump. When Orson drops us off I'm determined to get Billy on his own so I can give him a thorough grilling.

On the way, Orson starts on about some geezer he knows who went to New York and stepped into the wrong stretch limo. The man was beaten to a pulp with a cattle prod and thrown out of a moving car.

'Don't you think it was careless of him, Montse? Getting into a strange car like that?'

Billy's sitting up front, totally out of it, oblivious to Orson's threatening tone.

'They think I topped her,' he moans.

Orson ho ho's like Father Christmas, 'Oh, that's silly, Billy. You've got it all wrong. They're quite convinced she killed herself. They're just covering their backs. Interviewing everyone.'

'Have they interviewed you?' I ask.

Orson acts hurt. 'Why would they want to do that?'

Billy opens his eyes, 'Why would she want to kill herself?

She had everything going for her. She knew how to get whatever she wanted in life.'

Orson's failing to keep his voice in the same key as before. Shaking his head with unconvincing sympathy, he's trying to make eye contact with Billy while watching the road at the same time.

'Listen, son,' he says. 'You might have to start coming to terms with the fact that Gwendoline wasn't who you thought she was. I'm sorry, but if the police discover she's been creaming off council funds, say, and stashing money away in untraceable bank accounts in Guernsey, they might find a suicide motive in there somewhere. Money's gone missing, old chap. Finding it, of course, will be like looking for the proverbial needle in the haystack.'

Billy doesn't get it, 'But I already know Gwendoline wasn't who I thought she was,' he whines. 'I never really thought she was my mother, even though I knew, like, technically, she was.'

Off he goes, rambling on about his deprived childhood. Never had a proper holiday. Never this, never that.

'What about you, Ms Letkin,' Orson's turning to me. 'Did our friends succeed in unravelling your alibi?'

We're nearing a main railway station.

'No, they didn't.'

Leaning over, I poke Billy between his protruding shoulder blades.

'This is where we get out, mate. Will you let us out here, please, Mr Bainbridge?'

The heavy car rolls past the station and into a side street. Orson cruises along, taking his time about finding a place to stop.

'Gwendoline's frequent jaunts to Guernsey certainly seem to indicate that she had a strong interest in the place. Do you know what Guernsey is famous for?'

'Tomatoes?' Billy ventures.

'Their main commodity used to be tomatoes. But I doubt if Gwendoline went over there to sample their tomato crop. No, Billy, the twin source of their prosperity is banking and bonking. Your mother wasn't much interested in the latter. So perhaps she was making financial provision for your future, Billy. And who could blame her for putting a little bit aside for a rainy day in these uncertain times.'

We're almost going slow enough to climb out safely. The door handle won't budge though.

'Personally, I can't imagine Gwendoline had the necessary skills to manage an enterprise of that nature on a global financial scale. You'd need nerves of steel as well as having the right contacts.' Orson's continuing with his musings, giving the impression of thinking aloud, as he makes heavy weather of backing into a space wide enough to park a tank. Except, I know he's not thinking aloud. Every word of Orson's is chosen with care to make a certain impression on the listener. Set up future mental manipulations or put the frighteners on a poor little sap like Billy.

'Her talents lay elsewhere,' he says, as he positions the car. 'Perhaps she was threatened with exposure by a co-conspirator and, rather than be exposed, she chose suicide?'

He's looking through the back window, in my direction. Rashly, my big mouth flies open,

'Or perhaps a co-conspirator decided to go solo?'

'Good thinking, Ms Letkin. You may well be right!'

He thumbs a switch and the central locking system unclicks. Before I move, he's caught me by the wrist, pushing his face close to mine.

'Keep your nose out, Montse!'

My ankle twists painfully as I leap out of the car. Hobbling after Billy, I yell,

'See how he grabbed my wrist? See how he tried to force me to stay in the car?'

Billy ignores me, tottering along with his head lowered. When I catch up with him he's easily persuaded to come home with me. Matter of fact, persuasion doesn't even enter into it. He's an inert mass that just goes where it's pushed. A lot of people go through life that way. No volition. No gumption. No control over what happens to them. Moaners.

We've only been indoors a few minutes when the entryphone starts starting. Motor cycle messenger – huge gloves, goggles – with a letter from the council. Another grievance procedure. Karen alleges assault. A serious offence. After reading the letter I screw it in a ball and flick it at my guest. His arms flail the air and he flexes his legs with irritation. He's nothing but a screwed up, tight-arsed, little no-hoper. I feel like thumping him.

'How come Orson's on your case, Billy?'

'Orson's cool. He got me released didn't he? Everyone else is only looking out for number one. Orson's helping me get Gwendoline's will sorted out. That bitch owes me for fucking with my head. And I need Orson to get the council to sort out her pension stuff. He's given me a loan to tide me over till I can get my hands on some cash.'

Orson's been busier than I suspected.

'A loan? That's generous. How much?'

'A grand,' Billy says, pleased with himself.

That'll do nicely. I wish I could see the will, find out who the executors are and the beneficiaries, if any, besides the son and mother.

'Has Orson had access to the will?'

Adopting his unappealing, baffled look, Billy replies, 'Dunno. We go up her gaff and he must've taken some papers. He's cool, I told you. He's letting me use his solicitor to get the police off my back. Shit, Montse, I need someone on my side. What's the matter with that? I'm sick of fucking women telling me what to do. For once in my life I'm taking control. You don't know what shit my life's been. Whoever offed Gwendoline done me the best favour I could ever wish for. She never done me any. That's how I know she didn't top herself. She wouldn't want to give me and Gran the satisfaction.'

Me and Gran? His intense anger against Gwendoline comes out more in his incessant talking. He's so manic, and hate-filled, I'm beginning to wonder. Could he have killed Gwendoline? Gran might even have had a hand in it, the way he's talking. All this puts me and Maria in a different light. Her little stunt leaving me outside the shop and her jokes about anti-natal depression dwindle into insignificance.

Billy says 'Think I'm weird? Not feeling bad about Gwendoline carking it? Well, she didn't give a toss about me. She just went off and done her own thing!'

'Tell me more about your dealings with Orson. I know it pisses you off me saying so, but I don't trust that man. Did he ask you to sign anything? You didn't give him power of attorney or anything stupid like that? What's wrong with getting a second opinion? Let me see where she lived, have a poke through her stuff?'

The gentry muscled into this part of town in the eighties, then, in the nineties, got well hammered by negative equity. Today the place is going down the drain all over again. Every second house has an estate agent's sign hopefully stuck out front.

Vexed 'cause he's only been here once before and that was when he came with Orson, Billy's guiding me to his mother's house, soon to be his. All the time he'd been buried in the depths of rural idiocy, longing for the metropolis, Gwendoline was all on her own in this des res with its two-car OSP, tucked away behind strategically placed shrubbery. We're ambling across a vast unkempt lawn. With pinched nose and shaking fingers, Billy rattles a key into the front door. Orson must have obtained that key for him. By himself Billy couldn't organise pussy.

'Get the feeling we're being watched by a thousand eyes from behind lace curtains?' No answer. He's hunching his bony shoulders as we step into the hall, as if to withstand a blow.

'She never invited us here,' he says, booting the door shut. 'Not once. And the bitch never even gave us her phone number at home.'

'And now it's all yours, Billy'.

The ugliness of the front room is beyond belief. And I could swear there's a whiff of death hovering over the faded Laura Ashley gross-me-out sofa, frilly fat cushions and shag pile carpet.

All over the gaff – photos galore of Gwendoline – on the marble mantlepiece, on the entertainment suite and still more framed on the wall. Mostly snapped on election night. Partying at the Festival Hall as the news sank in, everyone sporting the trademark rictus grin. Gwendoline preening to camera, glutton dressed as glam, concealing the politics of envy within. Orson is captured in one of the pictures, standing to one side, observing her with an expression of unmistakable distaste.

An adjoining study's been trashed. Dust-free rectangles on a desk where computers and printers once sat. This small room's bristling with metal; desk, chairs, tubular shelving. Metal makes my teeth ache, especially when I'm nervous.

Glass doors open on to a long, ramshackle back garden. A grey dishevelled beehive appears above the wooden fence and is instantly retracted when the nosy neighbour sees

Billy, gone out through the back door, standing in the middle of the back garden, pissing into a bed of wormy nasturtiums.

And, oh, in the kitchen, a body. Dead cat, face buried in a dried saucer of Whiskas. Tail rigid as a poker. Poor moggy. What was your name? What would Gwendoline call her cat?

Orange slatted blinds on the kitchen windows have been lowered and shut tight. Gwendoline's aroma is everywhere, only slightly masked by smells of decay. Empty M & S boxes stewn on the table. Half eaten pizzas. Take-away trays choking up the sink.

Upstairs, in her monster bedroom, there's a bed that makes you throw up to look at, let alone sleep in. Hideous drapes covered in flounces of creamy satin. Bed the size of a footie pitch with ruffled pillows and knotted, none-too-clean sheets. The whole effect is causing the tiny hairs inside my nostrils to fibrillate madly. A sneezing fit's on its way.

In her walk-in wardrobe I have found a rack of designer threads, protected with plastic sheets and festooned with dry cleaning tags. She's got more shoes than Imelda Marcos, slung holus bolus in a pile also redolent of Imelda, but more like one of her rubbish tips. In fact the whole place exhibits surprising evidence of slobbishness. Obviously, old Gwendoline was not the domesticated type.

Her half-open knicker drawer exudes powerful sluttish smells. When I'm sorting through the rolled up balls of soiled pants she's stuffed back in the drawer along with clean ones, her presence becomes overwhelming. She's going to materialise. Her voice is right inside my ear, frozen breath on the tensors in my neck. Gritting my teeth, I continue, trying not to be disrespectful – like Trevor was with Weezie and Puja's stuff – in case, just in case, Gwendoline's watching. But, of course, what I'm doing is deeply disrespectful. When you think of her, a woman like Gwendoline, proud and powerful, protecting her secrets. And here's me, delving into her most intimate places, pushing my arm right in as far as it will go, like a veterinary midwife, right to the back of the drawer.

My palpating fingers encounter a rigid, book-shaped object – a video – *A Guernsey Diary*, the label says, narrated by Valerie Singleton. The box is heavier than it should be, though, and the lid pops open too easily when I put my thumb under it. Instead of a cassette inside, there's a filofax-style notebook, bursting with life, full as a club sandwich. Chiang's colleagues were careless. Perhaps, with their odd mixture of brutality and prissiness, their policeman's hands were repelled by what they had to touch.

eleven

'THE GP LOOKS AT my scar and says, "It's lovely and neat on the outside but who knows what kind of mess they've made inside".'

'For God's sake, Mum, can we talk about something else for a change?'

She's obsessed with her surgery and its after-effects: her bowel movements, wind in her system and her scar. And I've forced myself to listen to all this several times over. For a person like me, who can't stand sick people talking about their ailments, the whole business has been gross-out from the start though I've noticed in some strange way it's becoming less so. Phobia familiarisation therapy works for me. All the same my stomach's churning as she fumbles with her nightie.

'Oh no! Please don't show me!'

Once she spies the juicy bait I have to offer – Gwendoline's notebook, I'm confident of engaging her full attention. For a change I have to admit to a strange frustration, even disappointment, that her crusties – I refer to the people, not the scabby tissue encrusting her wound – have temporarily deserted her. Gone to burrow under roads in Devon, taking Weezie and Puja with them. I wish they were all here, especially Weezie, so they could witness my newly acquired magnetism – the result of procuring inside information in a high profile murder inquiry.

Hughie's at his post, still loyally attending to Maria's every whim. She's bored and needs a project. Poor Hughie's at a loss. A project is something he can't easily supply. I can. From now on directing her daughter's activities in the Gwendoline case will become her project.

At the moment she's specially receptive to hearing what's been happening with me. How I was picked up by the five-o, my visit to Gwendoline's house. She's horrified when I tell her about getting in the car with Orson.

'You said he wasn't dangerous!' I remind her, conscious of a pang at my own foolishness and trying to shift some of the responsibility on to her. Maybe I wasn't scared because I know that in reality none of this has got anything to do with me. I can stop my involvement at any time.

'I didn't tell you he wasn't dangerous,' she says, agitato. 'I distinctly remember saying that he gets others to do his dirty work for him.'

Apparently that wasn't always the case. Maria tells me me that when Orson was a student leader in the Young Socialists, she saw him pointing out militants to the police. Wearing his acid green steward's tabard, he'd start at the head of a march then drift back through the ranks, fingering comrades to the special branch accompanying the demo. Afterwards, the comrades compared notes and realised everyone who'd been arrested had been greeted by him briefly or had spoken to him shortly before. Orson himself was never arrested and never had a finger laid on him by the pork. Somehow I feel absolved as Mum tells me this. By contrast, I've never grassed up on a mate or done anything of the kind for political motives or out of malice or prejudice. No, I can say, hand on heart, there's no comparison between what Orson did, grassing up fellow students, and what I do, protecting the rights of the majority.

One of the students Orson grassed up was Red Gwen. Another was Matthew. Thanks to Orson they both achieved notoriety by turning their backs on the bourgeois court, refusing to recognise the authority of the bench. Back then, getting arrested was a status symbol among the middle classes. Not as good as getting the shit beaten out of you, but nevertheless an indispensable social asset.

'Around that time that Gwendoline would sign all her letters and articles "yours in armed love",' Mum says.

Hearing all this gets me thinking of Matthew's embarrassed reference to a fling between Mum and Orson. How could she let herself get taken in by such a tosser?

'But didn't you have a thing with Orson at one stage?'

'Who told you that?'

'Matthew.'

'God! I thought you were old enough to know that if a man like Orson wants to discredit you he spreads that kind of rubbish!'

Her mood improves when she sees me opening the notebook like a hamper full of goodies. One glimpse of Gwendoline's bold handwriting and Maria's slavering. Together we dissect my bloated, leatherbound bonanza, poring over our pickings. Doing something together for once and, to tell the truth, I need her help to make sense out of what I've found every bit as much as she needs a distracting crusade. By now, but for the Tory defectors who are still dewy-eyed, nearly everyone in the whole country has latched onto the fact that the Labour Party's crap. Maria pines for the days when her unique, insightful political analysis set her apart from others who had high hopes of a new Labour Government. She sorely misses her position at the leading edge. Evidently, I share her addiction to some form of insider knowledge; being first on the scene or, even better, illicit peeking behind the scenes.

Random notes, doodled as if for a future essay or diary are stuffed in the filobrain. Maybe Gwendoline was planning to write her memoirs?

'I only want to know the circumstances into which I was born. Is that so strange?'

Without us even noticing, Hughie has snuck into the room and sat himself down on the end of the bed.

'Since early childhood I've been aware of the startling contrast in every imaginable way; looks, temperament. My mother and I are so utterly dissimilar.'

Hughie startles us. 'Suicides are often nothing more than delayed infanticide.'

Yet another side to Hughie: Hughie the shrink.

'What the fuck are you talking about?' Maria demands.

'Just hear me out,' he says in a hoarse whisper, 'try to accept that inside everyone there's a place that remains unchanged since babyhood.' Me and Maria look at each other in alarm. 'It trusts, it knows no fear. Needs only to be loved. At an early age we learn that love isn't always returned. It has to be earned. This hurts, so we clam up and pretend we don't care. When we get older this prevents us from opening up to other people. We get anxious, lonely, depressed. Most uptight people were messed up by their childhoods.'

'Who are you blathering on about?' Maria shouts, causing cardiac palpitations under my ribs.

'Every child needs to know where he or she came from,' Hughie says firmly and stands up.

'Don't go, Hughie.' I squeak, snatching his fingers, afraid to be left alone with my angry mother, unable to face the discussion which might follow, the discussion we've never had and I've always wanted to have, though not like this.

Maria draws herself up on her cushions and whips up her nightie. Staring at me wildly she points to her vivid scar. 'This where *you* fucking come from and don't you forget it.'

Instinctively my hands go up to cover my face. Hughie touches my shoulder. 'OK, OK, it's OK to cry.'

'I'm not fucking crying!'

He bumbles off to make tea. Nothing a nice cuppa can't fix.

The manhole cover's clamped back over things. Under the lead-lined lid, feelings are sloshing around in a sickening fashion. Gratitude to Hughie for persisting with his probing; terror at what his nagging might bring forth. Family history's a seething can of worms. Just the sound of the F-word sends shivers down my spine and causes Maria to go into orbit. A conflagration may occur which will finish things off completely between me and my mother.

Hughie senses he's gone too far and, for now, he's decided to keep it buttoned.

Our silence is broken as Maria swoops on an advertisement which Gwendoline had ripped out of a newspaper and folded into the back pocket of the leather binder.

'Daughter of the late Evelyn Le Tissier wishes to meet friends and acquaintances of the Le Tissier family, tomato farmers, formerly of St Peter Port. Reply Box No.'

The late? Gwendoline has been suitably punished for consigning her mother to premature lateness.

From the pocket at the back of the book Maria's scavenging another fragment, this time a scrap of paper torn from a travel guide:

'Once the official residence of Guernsey's Governors, the Old Government House Hotel has served discerning visitors since 1858.'

'It looks to me as if Gwendoline may have been one of those discerning guests,' Maria says. Her eyes are closed like Mystic Meg and she's clutching the scrap of paper to her heart as if to squeeze out further information. 'I'm reminded of something. Something that happened in the Channel Islands. A Jewish woman was handed over to the SS.'

'What's that got to do with anything?'

'Shush, Montse, this is important!' flaps Hughie.

'The Channel Islands were occupied by the Germans during the war,' Maria goes on. 'A play about a woman called Therese Steiner caused a hell of a stink. A few years ago the authorities in Guernsey saw to it that the play couldn't be staged over there.'

According to Maria, the banned play was based on a true story. Therese had a big 'J' stamped in her passport in London whence she had fled to take up work as a nanny. She was obliged to accompany her misguided English employer to the 'safety' of the Channel Islands when war was imminent. When her boss realised the island was about to be invaded, she left, but Therese was held back to await the arrival of the occupation force, like an apple for the teacher. Constable Plod told her, 'You're a Jew. You belong to the Germans.' Once the Nazis landed the names of three women known to be Jewish were handed over and they were deported to Auschwitz, where they were all murdered.

So now we know how the Channel Islanders sucked up to the Germans in ways which, any moment now, Maria is sure to compare with what I do, even though there's no comparison. Like, it isn't me who calls the fraud hotline. I don't even answer the calls! In spite of all the gripes, we live in a democratic society. Government for the many, not the few. All I do is oil the wheels. You can't function without law and order. On the other hand, you have to have Fairness. The Nazis weren't fair and they weren't democratic. On the one hand this, on the other hand that. This and that are driving me nuts.

Gwendoline, self-referential as ever, has written the following memorandum to herself:

'I recognise that I'm vulnerable to the charge of collaboration myself. Although I can justify the underlying, long-term reasons behind all my decisions, I have to admit that I have implemented many distasteful policies, in some cases, policies which were total anathema to me and for which I have had to face the brickbats of those who, in my position, would behave no differently. The choices were made for me. One cannot fight on one's own.'

'Get Billy to take you to see the grandmother again. Can you?'

'Sure, I can get him to do anything. He's nothing but a dead twig that can be moved about and manipulated by whoever gets to him first. It's not that he's passive. He can be tetchy and nasty. But he's got no volition.'

'No volition, huh?'

Me and Orson are running neck and neck in the contest to influence Billy. But I like to think I'm edging slightly ahead. Or, has Orson lost interest in Gwendoline's son? Whatever Orson's up to, the boy in question, without undue duress, is taking me home for another chat with grandma. I wish I could say he came quietly. So long as I can get him to shut him up long enough for her to get a word in, she might shed some light on the notebook stuff. His main obsession today is ... Crash ... every time he get's his act together... Crash! Deprived of opportunity. Everything stacked against him.

He's rocking against his seat-belt. Gabbling. If only he'd been free to follow the career path of his choice he'd be a top film maker by now. He was just getting his portfolio together, when... *Crash!!*

After days of obsessing over comparative trivia, such as the exact amount of tobacco to mix with your grass, combined with uncontrolled pit stops at the temple of his expected inheritance, the big career theme turns up out of nowhere. Wound up to snapping, he's giving me a rundown on the crap work being done by this director and that director, name-dropping like there's no tomorrow. We make our way through traffic jams, speed along the M-way, from the centre of town right up to the gate of his grandmother's dilapidated house in the country.

Not even pausing to say hello or kiss-my-foot he's still obsessing as old Mrs Rhodes or whatever-her-name-is greets us at the door. She's pleased to see us. The kettle's bobbing merrily. And Maria suspects this harmless old geriatric was a pillar of the Third Reich!

Billy's upstairs digging out a video he wants me to watch. A collection of his master works. How to broach the subject of the stuff found in Gwendoline's diary? Billy doesn't know about finding the diary or that I took it, so I must tread carefully. Despite his self-centredness, you have to be careful. He's surprisingly acute when you least expect it. Once, out of the blue, he asked me a very personal question about my sexuality.

He's framed in the doorway, arms dangling.

'You can't see the film till I've done more work on it,' he says, sticking out his bottom lip. You'd think I'd given him a hard time, demanding to see his work, and his rejection of my request will utterly devastate me. So, I try to look devastated.

'Oh, no! Can't you let me have just one little peek?'

'I told you, it needs more work on it,' he says, sulkily, 'and I haven't got an editing suite. If I had an editing suite I'd be able to finish it and then you'd understand what I'm all about. You can't explain it in words. Words don't have the same power.'

'You water down your words by talking too much,' Gran says harshly, her Betty Crocker mask slipping momentarily. 'Your grandfather was an artist with words. His love letters to me are works of art.' Billy turns away, defeated, and drifts back upstairs. Addressing nobody, she declares, 'He doesn't realise it yet, but that's where Billy gets his artistic talent. From his grandfather.'

'Wow, I'm really interested in the art of letter-writing. Have you ever thought of getting those letters published?'

'They're very private,' she purrs, 'very special to me.'

'Great art's universal, it can be appreciated by almost everybody.'

Now, we're so close to talking about her wartime romance, I'm like a dog with an oily rag. 'Did Gwendoline get upset if you talked about your love affair with her father?'

The old woman nods, with a tragi-comic expression. Taking my cue from the radio counsellors people of Evelyn's generation apparently tune into in droves, I assure her gently but firmly, 'Gwendoline's gone now, she can't hurt you any more. And she can't chastise you for talking about your romance.'

Talk, you mad old bag! And talk she does. Now I know where Billy gets his garrulousness. Gwendoline's mother is unstoppable.

Old Evelyn was born on Guernsey just outside St Peter Port. Her parents grew tomatoes and kept a few cows. She was fifteen years old when the war started. Before school she used to cycle round the district delivering fresh milk. Back then there was no telly. Evelyn's parents sat by the radio trying to get news of the war situation. She wasn't scared. She felt secure because her parents were there, looking after her. What a nice feeling that must be. On that horrible night when I heard my mother's face being rearranged to resemble a painting by Picasso in his black and blue period, fear of all that could happen and the loneliness almost killed me.

Evelyn's parents had to make up their minds quick whether to stay on and pretend nothing was happening, or take up Churchill's offer of evacuation to England. Her mother took her down to the evacuation boats three times and each time they were turned back in the mêlée. The port was choked with ships and the ships were ramjam to the gunnels. People packed like cattle, clutching their pathetic bundles and suitcases, in boats normally used to haul coal or potatoes. All over the place Evelyn saw notices saying 'don't be yellow, stay!'

Separated from her mother, she sat on her suitcase waiting for a bus that never came, glad she was still on the island but terrified by the scene at the quayside. People were desperately trying to sell their cars for a pound but no one would buy, even for a penny. Lines of abandoned motors banked up. Pets couldn't be taken. Evelyn had been devastated when she overheard a vet friend telling her father how he had put down 8,000 dogs in one day.

Bowing her head, she continues narrating her story in a rehearsed fashion, as if attuned to the tiny microphone hidden in my pocket, an impulse-buy from Spymaster.

'On a warm summer's day I was playing in the street with my friends. Out of a clear blue sky, planes appeared over the water, coming in low over the harbour. We waved to them. They were so low we could see the pilots. Machine gun bullets streamed into the streets.'

'We hid down the steps of a neighbour's house until it was safe to go home. A few days later we saw columns of German soldiers marching down the road.'

Evelyn kept an open mind about the Germans. 'They were only human beings, like us,' she tells me, half petulant, half defiant.

'My first contact with them was when they rolled up in an armoured car and parked it at the farm. I was shaken when I saw how nervous my father was.'

'How did you meet your, er, Gwendoline's father?'

'Oh, we had a special relationship right from the beginning,' she says, 'Heinrich and me. A love-match made in heaven. I treasure his beautiful letters. Sheer poetry. He gave his life for his country, you know, and I'm not supposed to talk about him.

'I'd just turned seventeen. I met him at a village dance. The German boys were forbidden to dance. It would have been shameful while fellow soldiers were being killed on the front line. Of course I noticed him as soon as he came into the room. He was nineteen years old, fit, blond, blue eyes. Smartly pressed uniform. An *unteroffizier*, the equivalent of a sergeant. He swept me off my feet.

'The local boys hated us going with German soldiers. They were jealous of their good looks and the power they had. We got called a few nasty names. But, at the time, there was no serious backlash. By the third year of the occupation things had softened towards the troops. They'd be going up and down the streets, buying things from shops, coming on farms to buy produce and make conversation. We were on an island. We couldn't go away. No one knew if they were going to die tomorrow, or what would become of them in the future.'

Heinrich's comrades had mined the beaches against a

British attack that never happened. He knew the safe places to go for a bit of the other.

'We skipped hand in hand through the bluebells or lay on a cliff top at sunset, listening to the sound of waves breaking on the beach. We talked for hours.'

A Mills and Boon idyll passes before my eyes with Dennis Potter sex scenes between the daffy little blonde from behind Boots' counter and her soldier boy. That's the way Evelyn's presenting it, yet from her tone of voice you can tell she was an empathiser. She admired the Kraut way of doing things.

She goes on, 'He told me that when he was a young boy the film Ben Hur was very popular. Silent, before the talkies. Boys played chariot games, pretending to be Ramon Novarro, opposing teams of anti-Nazis or Nazis, bumping into each other and knocking each other to the ground. When the Hitler Youth spread, only Nazi chariots were allowed. Children painted swastikas on their desks and girls painted swastikas on their fingernails and shouted "Heil Hitler" in class. Children spontaneously demanded colonies. No prompting at all! You see, Miss Letkin, France and Britain had colonies and Germany had missed out. That wasn't fair, was it?

'Heinrich was such a softie, he was upset because he'd seen the bodies of young men hanging from lamp posts with placards labelled "I am a coward" around their necks. They had refused to join the army. Conchies. There was no place for them in the new Germany.'

My hands quake as I imagine those boys, long dead. I am a coward! I am a coward! But old Evelyn has moved on.

'One girl I knew thought she was a very clever miss, flying about on her bicycle turning her nose up. Cycling past as if the soldiers weren't there. They went to her house when she was playing the piano for guests. As they passed through the room she played the Laurel and Hardy signature tune thinking they wouldn't recognise it, but one of them did. She got off lightly for insulting an officer. Got away with a £10 fine. Of course, it was a lot of money in those days. But compared to what happened to some people who misbehaved, it was nothing.'

Shortly after Christmas, 1944, Evelyn discovered she was pregnant. Heinrich had been sent to the Russian front from whence, I assume, he penned his allegedly poetic letters.

The eleven months between D-day and VE-day were rough for the islanders. The allies had liberated France, cutting off supplies to the German garrison on the Channel Islands. Heinrich's letters ceased to arrive. People were eating all kinds of shit. Even their pets.

'We were left in the lurch by Churchill. Do you know what he said? "Let 'em rot." That's what he said about the Channel Islands!'

Just in time, a Red Cross supply ship arrived from Portugal.

'I nearly called Gwendoline "Vega" after the boat,' Evelyn smiles. 'We were so happy we could eat real food again. But so many others called their girl babies Vega I wanted to be different.'

For the first time I think of Gwendoline as a baby, small and helpless as Puja, needing everything done for her. And this was the woman who changed her pooey nappies, heard her first words and watched her take her first steps.

'Enemy planes were going over to attack. Scores and scores of them roaring over for hours and hours on end.'

'Enemy? You mean the Luftwaffe?'

'No,' she says irritably, 'I'm talking about the RAF. Let me tell it in my own way. Where was I? Yes, I had to give up my job as a seamstress shortly after I knew I was expecting. Guernsey wasn't liberated until May.'

'What was that like?'

'Aha! That was when all the trouble started, after the wretched liberation. The champagne and silk-stocking floozies who went with the officers and were blatant about it, gave the rest of us a bad name. High-up officers were all aristocrats, von-this-and-von-that, who couldn't even tie their own shoe laces. The girls who went with them put on airs and graces but they were nothing better than common prostitutes. A lot of them were French. Some of those whores were tarred and feathered. One had a cloth dipped in petrol put between her legs and set fire to.'

Charming!

Even though Evelyn had told me that she herself had tried to get on the evacuation boats she was nasty about people who 'just skipped off to England'. Some evacuees never came back. Or came back and slagged off those who'd remained for not putting up a fight.

'What could we do?' Evelyn says. 'We were just a little island.'

Even the head of the Guernsey Government, Victor Carey, with the grisly title of Bailiff, was accused of collaborating. Evelyn excuses him.

'He was a weak man. But, by God, he kept the peace. He kept us safe. Irresponsible provocateurs were making things difficult for everyone. Silly kids acting the goat, letting down tyres, releasing handbrakes on armoured vehicles. The Bailiff offered good money, £25 apiece, for information on children who went around at night painting V-signs on walls. Not one Guernseyman was shot for sabotage. Not one! And Victor received a knighthood at the end of the war.

'Once on television I saw an old man being put on trial for what they call war crimes. But the TV people asked his neighbours and they all said he was a lovely old man. A real gentleman. He played with their children.

When I saw that man I thought "he could have been my Heinrich".'

Remembering what my mother had written to me, that I was a courageous child, I'm more interested in hearing about the children who went out at night painting slogans. What else did they get up to? I'm having a daydream in which I am a munchkin leading a band of smaller munchkins, on a breathtaking march, shoving swastika-tagged trucks over a cliff, painting anti-Nazi slogans on the sea wall.

Evelyn's still talking.

'We wouldn't have had so much trouble in the colonies if we'd given them the Channel Islands system,' she opines. 'Why do you think so many ex-pats from Rhodesia and Kenya and other parts of Bongobongoland have settled there?'

'I'm sure you're going to tell me, Evelyn.'

'Because they need a safe haven for their capital, that's why.'

Her eyes bug out of her head when I ask her if she knew about the Jewish women handed over to the Nazis by the Guernsey police.

'All the Jews had left before the war. But if they were still there, then they were stupid!'

My usual reaction to alternative explanations of historical or scientific phenomena is either to believe the alternative or, at least, try my best to believe it. Isn't that better than accepting the brain-deadening tripe served up by the mainstream for the edification of the masses? Self-education reveals that the 'black hole' of Calcutta was one of those dodgy atrocity stories dreamed up when imperialists want an excuse to take over someone else's country.

Just prior to the Battle of Plassey in 1757, the East India Company's defences were breached by the Nawab of

Bengal. Their man in Calcutta, John Zephania Holwell, had to surrender his sword to a 'native'. Drunken British soldiers broke the ceasefire and attacked some of their conquerors who promptly complained to the Nawab. The drunks, along with Holwell, were locked up in the local East India Company jail for the night. Around sixty went in, next morning only twenty-three came out, among them, Holwell. He makes out he's a superhero. Survives three gruelling days of battle, a night in the 'black hole' buried under 'hundreds' of bodies, then fettered, marches all next day, in scorching, searing sun. Even 'Clive of India' didn't believe it. The incident was spun for consumption back in Blighty before Plassey and the big-time atrocities which followed. Records declare Holwell alive and well a month later, business as usual, at the East India Company's Madras office.

Nothing more was heard of the 'black hole' until fifty years on when Holwell's version provided juicy material for imperialist hagiologies. The 'hole' grew so large that, along with the 'Indian Mutiny', it became one of the things 'every schoolboy knows' about India. Now it's ingrained in the national consciousness: Whenever the lights go out it's, 'Oo-er, it's like the Black Hole of Calcutta in here.'

Something I saw on the box late one night convinced me the Apollo landings were faked in a studio. People believed because they'd seen it on TV. Heard the one-small-step-for-mankind rap. The deniers pointed to shadows going in wrong directions. Light where no light source existed. How could they have penetrated the Van Allen belt and returned in such a puny craft? Where was the photographer standing who took the picture of Neil Armstrong coming down the ladder? Like, what was God standing on when he or she created the Universe?

Sat here listening to this holocaust-denying, septuagenarian flat-earther, far from exciting my thirst for alternative versions of history, she's giving me the dry heaves.

My autodidactic method consists of flitting from shelf to shelf like a greedy magpie collecting gaudy baubles. Dull little islands off Britain's shores held no attraction. Beefy men in yachting caps was all I'd gleaned from bookshelves by a process of osmosis. Acting on Maria's orders, though, Hughie has been far more methodical. He has returned from the newspaper library with a booty which, while it could never equal mine in authenticity, is nevertheless a rich catalogue of banking and bonking. By the time I arrive back at the squat the pair of them have gorged themselves on information.

Ave Maria's one of those people who, when it comes to any subject under the sun remotely connected to what she claims as *her* territory; namely Politics, she's been-there-done-that. Now she's an expert on the Nazi occupation of the Channel Islands. Even though I'm the one who's been there and done that: namely, sat in Evelyn's kitchen for hours on end acquainting myself with the minutiae of wartime life on Guernsey. In case anyone wants to know they rolled fags from dried turnips, fucked or ate anything that moved, made soup out of cows turds, clothes out of curtains and learned *Hoch Deutsch* in their spare time.

'Look at all this stuff about Jerrybags.' Mum's holding up a sheaf of front pages painstakingly photocopied by Hughie. 'What I think happened was, Gwendoline suspected that her mother was one of these slags who slept with the enemy. The poor fucking woman had to face the fact that in all probability she was a spore of Hitler!'

They don't need me! They don't need my tape. Maria and Hughie have cracked the code for themselves, just by putting two and two together and getting four. Maria doesn't need me to confirm what she knows. She's as entirely lacking in self doubt as I thought, until recently, Gwendoline had been.

More and more details of the Nazi occupation of the Channel Islands were made public from the mid-nineties onwards. According to Maria's reckoning, this would have placed Gwendoline under more and more pressure to face up to reality. She could ignore her Channel Island connections no longer. Once the fifty-year gagging order lapsed in 1995, and on every anniversary after that, year on year the Public Record Office would disgorge more and more previously secret files.

Just before the war broke out, Britain declared the islands 'open' but forgot to tell the Germans. They asked Joseph P. Kennedy who was American ambassador at the time to use his contacts to inform the Germans. Maybe he did, maybe he didn't. Whatever, when war was declared the Luftwaffe was sent in.

'*Blood mingled with tomato pulp on the wharf where boxes of fruit awaited shipment to England.*'

The raid on Guernsey lasted fifty minutes. Bombs were falling and machine-gun bullets streamed into the streets. *Blood mingled with tomato pulp*, Hughie reads in a reverent whisper.

Evelyn's information was correct. The cuttings confirm that the Bailiff did get a knighthood after the war even though he'd issued proclamations referring to allied troops as 'enemy forces', organised deportations of hundreds of British-born people to camps in mainland Europe and helped send Jews to their deaths in the gas chambers of Auschwitz and Dachau.

Maria reads out some of the grovelling letters which had lain unseen in the Public Record Office for fifty years and were now opened up to the light of day. Some of them have been tampered with, names covered up, out of respect for the living. Others are under lock-and-key until 2045. Maybe I'll be still around – Puja will be middle-aged.

'Dear Feldkommandantur, I have the honour to report the Order which accompanied your letter was communicated to the Royal Court. I can assure you there will be no delay in furnishing you with the information you require.' – i.e. names of Jews.

Deportees names were grouped under three helpful headings. 1) Jews, 2) politically unreliable, 3) workshy.

Ambrose Sherwill CBE became Bailiff in 1946 and was knighted in 1949. He was President of the Guernsey Controlling Committee during the war.

According to Victor and Ambrose, *'To get away or attempt to get away is a crime against the local population.'*

British raiding parties weren't welcome either. Sherwill told his policemen what to do if special operations men landed on Guernsey clandestinely.

'However detestable the duty of reporting the presence of strangers in our midst, I see no way of avoiding it.'

The only Nazi commandment Carey and Sherwill could really get worked up about was the one from the Feldkommandantur demanding the liquidation of the Freemasons lodges.

'It would be asking a lot of those members of the legislature who are Freemasons to violate their undertakings by voting their associations out of existence.'

'See?' Maria cries, gobbling up newsprint by the yard, 'Gwendoline's fixation could only be satisfied by a trip down memory lane. And memory lane is closed to the public for major reconstruction! Oh, they rewrote history within twenty-four hours.

'Wartime culture is one of the great myths of our time: ad nauseam pap; fantasy. Biggles, Dambusters, laughing through the tears, hanging out your knickers on the Siegfried Line, the Dame with the mythical name, Nark of

Sark. Nothing about the great anti-fascist united front between the Soviet Union, Britain and the United States.'

There's something I've always wanted to ask and now seems a good moment,

'Hey, Mum, If everyone in England were such great anti-fascists, how come things turned out the way they have?'

Instead of ranting and raving like she usually does, Maria adopts her guru voice, as if I was one of her acolytes. Strangely, I find this soothing and follow her words intently,

'The united front worked fine during the war but after 1945 the Yanks and the British were more interested in destroying the Soviet Union than they were in denazification. They half-heartedly went through with the Nuremburg trials leaving Nazi lawyers, teachers and army officers free to run West Germany for the duration. Read D.N. Pritt!'

Apparently Maria and Hughie weren't as confident about their historical reconstruction as they'd made out. They're agog when I tell them I taped all the stuff about Heinrich, swastikas on fingernails, and Ben Hur.

'Jaysus, why didn't you say you had a tape before instead of sitting there like a constipated camel?'

They listen spellbound, interrupting to play it again when Evelyn's words are indistinct, leaning forward, 'What did she say?'

And because I was there I can distinguish the bits that are hard to recognise. We come to the place when Evelyn says, *His neighbours said he was a lovely old man. A real gentleman. He played with their children.*

'Neighbours! Doody, doody, doody, doo-dah! Fucking neighbours,' Maria shouts, 'What about Joy Gardner? They said she was too big, too loud, too black. I'll bet her fucking neighbours wished they lived next to a lovely old Nazi like that.'

Impatient, I stop the machine to tell them the best bit! 'Evelyn said there weren't any Jews left on the Channel Islands when the Germans turned up but if there were, then they were stupid!'

Encouraged by the accuracy of her speculations so far, Maria's now constructing a scenario in which the finger of suspicion points to Orson. Orson's guilt is, in fact, a foregone conclusion.

'If Gwendoline topped herself, I'll eat my keks,' she threatens, building on the story as she goes along. 'Orson's been stashing money in a bank account on Guernsey and he freaks out when Gwendoline starts going back and forth. He's thinking she's caught him out. Then, oh so conveniently, she ups and croaks just like that? No one's going to tell me she topped herself just because her father was a Nazi. In this day and age she'd probably get a medal.'

'Couldn't it be the other way round?' Hughie asks innocently. 'Orson might've found her out and might have been trying to extort money from her? Just because she was researching her family history doesn't mean she wasn't laundering money too. Maybe she cracked under pressure and jumped.'

Maria rounds on him, not missing a beat, her futon overflowing with papers.

'You don't know these people like I do,' she roars, 'Gwendoline was too politically ambitious to risk everything. The ultimate careerist. You need to meet Matthew. He'll give you the background.'

Wasn't Gwendoline past it? Nearing retirement?

'People like that never give up,' Mum says. 'Matthew will tell you.' But I can't help thinking if Matthew's so fucking smart, how come he's been living in a stinking B & B half his life?

Still reading, Maria's all excited, planning how she's going to bring old and new comrades together; thinking aloud, making plans for Hughie and Matthew to meet, when suddenly the talk stops. She reads silently.

'What is it?' Hughie asks.

'It says here two hundred letters a week poured into the headquarters of the German high command from islanders denouncing their neighbours for petty infringements of the Nazi penal code. God, Hughie, what does that remind you of?'

My heart takes a dive. She's getting at me again just as I'm starting to feel accepted and part of something. Is the shit going to descend? But she isn't looking at me. She's looking past me, over my shoulder at someone who's standing there.

'Gotcha,' says Cheeseface, pushing forward with her hands on her hips. 'I knew I'd come across you sooner or later. Everybody? Say hello to Mary, a fucking grass who works for the council.'

A group of crusties have barged in. Weezie is with them, Puja on her back. His eyes are seeking me out, glowing with recognition and intelligence. I can see why Weezie says 'he's an old soul'.

My mother's features sag like deflated latex. Weezie recovers first.

'Glenys,' she says reasonably, 'I think you'll find you're making a mistake over this. This is my friend. I went to school with her. I've known her for years. Montse would never grass up anyone. Yes, she works for the council, but she helps tenants. You've got it all wrong. Her name isn't Mary. Her name's Montse Letkin. She's Maria's daughter.'

Not knowing what else to do, I try to act like nothing's happened, ignoring Cheeseface-Glenys. But she's not letting me get away with it. She immediately takes charge, before Mum gets a chance to open her mouth.

'We need a meeting about this as a matter of urgency. This is a serious breach of security. Hughie, you keep an eye on Mary, or whatever her name is. Don't let her leave the premises.'

Hughie's almost crying.

'You're responsible for security, Hughie, just do it,' Glenys commands and sweeps out.

Hughie puts his hands on my shoulders, 'Why don't you leave, Montse,' he says. I look at Weezie to see if she's making a move to follow me. 'Louise and the baby are staying.' Hughie says out loud, then he whispers, 'I'll be in touch.'

What choice do I have?

twelve

THE NOVELTY OF BEING snugly included evaporates into the ether the instant Cheeseface denounces me, her challenge left hanging in the air. Dazed as if from a physical blow, I retreat immediately.

I hereby dedicate my life to the overthrow of Cheeseface, the blagger who exploded my only chance of restoring good relations with my mother, who humiliated me in front of my one and only friend and who revived the dead issue of my job. I will bash in her head, crunch her bones, stomp all over her face. My hands are shaking. I can't be still, pacing the room like a caged animal, pounding the walls, full of loathing for my gorgeous gaff. Without Weezie and Puja it's a dead zone. No point to anything. I was radio rental to get so attached. Girls at school used to say I was possessive when I let them get too close. Then they'd drop me from a great height and run off laughing.

Yesterday I was on top of the world. How different my life might have been if Cheeseface did not exist! If only Gwendoline had lived and thrived and promoted me according to her plan. Now I'm double gutted. If only I could crawl into a hole and never come out. Thoughts of delayed infanticide, as defined by Hughie, creep inside my skull and take roost there. A decision must be made as to whether to drink myself senseless or top myself by more immediate means. I'm resigned to doing the former – the time is 9 p.m. and my hand is on door of the refrigerator – when the entryphone starts tooting. Whoever it is ain't English. English people don't ring doorbells of an evening without phoning first. And I don't wanna see nobody. But the ringing doesn't stop.

'Who's it?'

'Joe.'

'Joe who?' His groans of annoyance balloon out of the instrument, amplifying into my space, doing my head in. At the same time he's got his finger on the buzzer, collapsing my resistance. Taking his shoes off in the hall he looks bewildered by my less-than-enthusiastic welcome.

'Whaddya want?'

'I just want to talk, Montse, off the record. Hey, nice place,' he says poking his head into the living room.

'Is this the first time you've been here?'

'Ye-es,' he says warily.

'So you say!' implying he might've been before on a secret police visit.

'I told you it wasn't us,' he protests. 'Don't you think your girlfriend would have mentioned seeing me?'

'She ain't my girlfriend!'

Now he's on the sofa, neat little feet tucked under him. I'm on a low chair beside the stereo sorting through a box of cassettes, trying to blank him, carefully doing nothing to improve the atmosphere.

Minutes jangle by. Me getting on his nerves, clattering cassettes like castanets. His cheeks bunch as if he's sucking a lime and he's constantly changing his position on the sofa. Up till now in all my dealings with Joe I've been too sycophantic, overly flattered by his attention. The sudden change in my manner registers on his expressive face. Deadpan ain't his style. He's uncomfortable. He came here for a heart to heart and now, because of my new prickliness, he can't decide how to behave.

Without the aid of alcohol I'm having difficulty meeting his gaze, keeping myself busy playing tunes. This one's too brash; change to mellow, but that's too depressing. So I'm trying one tune after another.

He pulls down the corners of his mouth and two stern lines appear between his eyebrows.

'Just leave one thing on for two minutes, can't you?'

Rage bursts my wafer-thin veneer of control. 'You can fuck off if you don't like it. Who invited you here anyway?'

Without a word he gets up and starts jiggling the door handle.

'Oh, for fuck sakes, Joe, siddown and tell me about it.'

He sits. 'I thought you and me were on the same wave length, Montse. You're the one who put the idea in my head that Orson was a bad one. You convinced me he was a candidate for prime suspect.'

Music to my ears!

'Instead of taking my input on board,' Joe says, 'my chief has completely rubbished me. I'm off the case for suggesting Orson's a villain.'

He's throwing caution to the wind. Telling me how the stupid gavvers are making a pig's ear of Gwendoline's case. Swearing me to secrecy.

'It seems as though my bosses are only going through the motions of conducting an inquiry. Something stinks. We're not even a hundred per cent sure which balcony she dived off,' he says, hushed by the admission. 'She might have gone over from the floor above, or she might have gone over from the floor below. We just don't know. Security was slack. Evidence got contaminated.'

'What about Orson?'

Joe laughs.

'Orson's got the chief eating out of his hand. He's got

us running round in circles till we're disappearing up our own backsides. Came to us with his own story before we even got round to interviewing him. Said he suspected Gwendoline was on the take. Everything fitted in with what we already knew. According to the travel agent, she went over to Guernsey at least four times in two years. Orson says he confronted her about her activities. Acts terribly upset. Blaming himself. We're meant to draw the conclusion that she killed herself because he rumbled her. He's managed to convince my chief that his intervention triggered her suicide. Even offered his expert services to the fraud squad to help them trace the missing money. How you set up companies, buying off the shelf, all the ins and outs of how to sort yourself out a little off-shore company. In a back-handed way everything he said was framing Gwendoline. And they bought it. No kidding, the Ministry of Funny Handshakes might be involved.'

Why's Joe telling me this? Either he suspects I know more and there's something I'm not telling him or the little plonker needs some kind of favour. The man admits the police had uncovered the hidden tape recorder before I went and told them what I'd found. They'd already listened to the tape, heard my silly phone calls and were waiting to see what I'd do next. Joe was on my tail. He says he's sorry he lied to me.

'But I did tell you I believed you, didn't I? That's what I thought was important. To let you know that you were believed.'

'But it was all lies, Joe!'

My assumption that Orson gave the tape to the police was completely wrong. So what else have I misread? Maybe I've been over-eager to please Maria, using wishful thinking to put Orson in the frame. Joe's deception about the tape makes me feel like I don't want to share the Channel Island stuff with him and yet it would be so neat if Orson could be nailed by our combined efforts.

If I share the information about the Channel Islands and Joe solves the case, he'll take all the credit. How can I get him to cut me in on his unofficial investigation? Maria would break with me for good if she heard I was co-operating with the five-o. On the other hand, if Joe's prepared to go for it in his own time and if we succeed in pointing the finger at Orson, Maria would forgive anything and Joe would be vindicated.

'Those crooked, racist bastards are never going to accept me. They're going to block my career forever.' He jabs the fist of one hand into the palm of the other. 'Maybe I should pack it all in and go into the restaurant business. But I love what I do and I'm damn good at it!'

Which way would Maria jump on that? Hard one to call. In the past she's scoffed at cases brought by gays in the military or women in the old bill. According to her they deserve all they get for joining the enemy. But she'd eat shit to see Orson behind bars.

Besides, Joe's educated. Got degrees 'n that.

'Don't throw it all away, Joe. Make them recognise you.'

Joe and me've got common cause. Both of us would improve our positions in life if we pooled our resources and sorted Gwendoline's case. My dearest hope – to redeem myself, might be achievable after all.

'Have you talked to Gwendoline's mother?'

'What? That old bimbo? Why should I?'

'What if I told you that Gwendoline's trips to Guernsey were all about Eve? Nothing to do with laundering money? I've got evidence!

'See, Gwendoline's father was a kraut. When the Nazis occupied the Channel Islands during the war, he was stationed there for the duration. This Nazi knocks up Evelyn, who was a teenager at the time. Then he's shipped off to the Russian front where he croaks, or does he? We've only got Evelyn's word for it – he might still be strutting around somewhere in Germany or even back on Guernsey. Lots of them went back, they loved it so much. Hitler had great plans for turning the islands into resorts for the Strength through Joy movement.'

'Cut it out, Montse, all this is totally off the planet.'

'You wanna know why Gwendoline was going over there or not?'

'Sure, but just remember, not everybody's interested in Piddle-on-the-Marsh. Europe isn't the centre of the universe.'

'Okay, okay, I didn't say it was! Bloody Jesus, don't be so touchy. I'm just telling you what Gwendoline was trying to find out. She goes over there to research her family history. She doesn't trust her mother's version. Mills and Boon had nothing on Evelyn. You should hear the way she waffles on about her blue-eyed, Jack-booted Nazi boy.'

'Are these islands part of Britain or what?'

'They're a dependency with a local parliament.'

I'm giving Joe the version of events cobbled together by Maria, myself and Hughie from newspaper cuttings and confirmed by Evelyn's own story. Gwendoline didn't kill herself and she certainly didn't kill herself out of shame. She'd suspected about her father for some time and she was building up a picture of life under the Nazi occupation, trying to work out what happened to her mother and what happened to other women who got involved with the Germans.

'I guess she needed to know where she came from.' I find myself repeating Hughie's mantra: everybody has this place inside blah, blah.

Joe's aghast. 'Montse, where'd you pick up all this new age crap?'

New age crap? Now it's me who's aghast. I didn't know

it was new age crap. To me it was all original. I thought Hughie'd thought it up for himself. Why can't I keep it zipped? Showing myself up in front of Joe! He hones in on phoniness in like a fucking Exocet. We get diverted into an argument about whether or not it's OK to call Germans krauts. I say it is. Joe says it ain't.

Several cans of beer later he asks, 'If you're so damn sure of all this, why not put it to the test? If you get a result, I'll go along with it.'

'What can I do?'

He just happens to have Orson's mobile number about his person.

'Call him up and tell him you've got something to sell him. Tell him you've found something about Gwendoline's death that might be to his advantage. See if you can get a meeting.'

Oh, no, man! Joe can do his own shit! Maybe he'd prefer the drunken plan I hatched with Maureen. Raid the therapist's van in the dead of night and steal Gwendoline's records.

'In a way, I prefer you don't tell me,' he says with a straight face, 'as a police officer, I really can't condone illegal break-ins.' Then he giggles and I know he's joking.

'There'd be an awful lot of insecure neurotics around if news of that plan ever got out. You two'd put the psycho-bus out of business. My idea's more likely to succeed.'

Will Orson be that easy to freak? I'm doubtful but Joe's persuasive. He goes to his car to get a recording device to attach to the phone which will bring Orson's voice out into the room – 'say you discovered a bank account she was using or a diary, something the police missed.'

'That's too complicated.'

'OK. Try an anonymous call. Get him worried. See what he says.'

I dial the number a couple of times and slam the receiver

down giggling like a bubblehead. On the third try I let it ring. We hear Orson catch his breath.

'You're demented. Stop harassing me or I'll call the police. Is it because you're so unattractive that you have to resort to shock tactics to get my attention?'

I'm slamming down the receiver.

'I think the bastard recognised my voice.'

After the phone call, we both feel more upbeat though I'm still vexed that it's me who has to carry out the dirty work. Joe keeps nagging me to ring again.

'It's too late.'

'What the fuck? Who cares what time it is? What are we doing here, arranging a tea party? We want to give him the jitters. The later you ring the better. After midnight's the most effective time.'

My brain's seething with ruses. Anything to delay. I want to know, am I a born informer? I appeal to Joe's expertise, his insider knowledge. Does he think there's a gene that produces us snitches? He tells me he has to work with informers every day. None of them are nice people. Not the sort he'd have dinner with or drop in on without a prior arrangement to shoot the breeze. Does this mean he sees me in a different light from the paid informers he deals with? Is our relationship different? Is it the question of the cash payment that makes it different? The informers on the Channel Islands were not all paid. Most of them did it not for financial reward but for the satisfaction of settling old scores.

'Please search 45 Ingreville Terrace for radio transmitters hidden under floorboards and in walls. Good luck. I hope you catch the bastard.'

Casting around for further distractions I remember, I

didn't play Joe the tape I made of Evelyn. I still have it in my pocket. Wouldn't he like to hear it?

'What a tinny sound,' he complains. Reminds him of hearing on the radio the first sound recording ever made. Thomas Edison testing his own invention. Joe heard him reciting 'Mary Had a Little Lamb'. Why recite that garbage? Wouldn't you think a man with a brilliant mind like that could think of something better to say?

'His engineers asked him to say something and that's the first thing that came into his head,' Joe says, irritably.

'Well, this one's called Evie had a little kraut,' I say, slotting my tape in the machine. We listen for five minutes and then Joe reaches over and switches the machine off. Fucking cheek!

'Quit stalling,' he says, 'and make that call!'

'OK, OK, I'll do it. Just let me get my head around it.'

How much confidence do I actually have in Maria's theory of Orson as murderer? Fifty-fifty? Someone offed Gwendoline. I'm sure of that. Follow my instinct! Gamble the lot; my self-esteem and my status in the world with everyone I care about. I've got nothing to lose and could be vindicated for good'n all. Is it just a matter of picking up the phone and making that call? Without a breakthrough I'm back to the old life of dealing this'n that to scrape a living. For Joe the alternative's joining the family business, waiting tables in Soho. Failure. 'They're all waiting for me to fail. They hate me being a policeman,' Joe whines.

Does he know the stain of collaboration? Does he feel it as a cop? I'd like to ask but it might be a touchy subject; might spoil our relationship, if you could call our strange comradeship a relationship. What kind of ship is this?

I am a coward. When surveilling powerless people I'm full

of confidence. Playing telephone tricks; ringing doorbells; but the idea of attempting to entrap a professional, high-profile wheeler-dealer like Orson fills me with terror. Yet it's my only chance for redemption. Joe, too, is pinning his hopes on me. He thinks I owe him something for listening to my story. He hasn't said so but that's the implication. I can sense his resentment that he listened to me in the first place. Who asked him to stick his big neck out? But without my drunken repetitions of Maria's theory, Joe would never've felt so certain that Orson was worth pursuing.

Tempus fugit and I want Joe to go now. The man's getting boring. Monosyllabic, weary and bleary, settling down on my sofa and assuming he can stay the night. To get him to leave I agree to make another telephone call. One last attempt at ensnaring Orson, although I believe I'm behaving beyond the call of duty. Why not leave it till tomorrow? Suddenly I'm so tired I don't give a fuck. What harm can Orson do me down the phone? Make the call then throw Joe out.

I pick up the receiver. Suddenly Joe perks up.

'Wait! Listen to this. How about telling him the story you told me? Tell him you broke into the therapist's van and nicked Gwendoline's records. Tell him Gwendoline told her shrink everything. She told her shrink she'd seen Orson and one of his minions on Guernsey and she suspected they were there on a money laundering expedition.'

It works. Joe punches the air and shouts 'Yes!'

I'm to meet Orson tomorrow at Heathrow.

At last Joe's gone and I'm in the bathroom throwing up lozenges of solid green bile.

La Gazette Officielle

A reward of £25 will be given to the person who first gives to the inspector of police information leading to the conviction of anyone (not already discovered) for the offence of marking on a gate, wall, or any other place visible to the public the letter V or any other sign or any word or words calculated to offend the German authorities or soldiers.
This day of July 1941,
Victor G. Carey, Bailiff"

If I'd been there when I was a kid, would I have been painting V-signs or collecting twenty-five quid?

Orson keeps glancing at the CCTV monitor. He hasn't seen me yet, not that I'm hiding. Only holding back out of slight nervousness. What can go wrong in front of an airport full of witnesses with armed security guards patrolling the concourse?

People bunch in groups near the arrivals channel watching a young guy in a kurta and baggy pants pushing a trolley loaded with canvas bags, bongs and brassware, stoned out of his brains. He's blinking under the strip lighting then walking the gauntlet with us all staring at him. He looks how I feel.

Orson's waiting for me in the Harvester Bar. All he's carrying is a camel-hair coat and a padded laptop bag. Has he checked his luggage through already? His blonde tresses have been freshly brushed. Floppy on top, short back and sides. He's relaxed and *soigné* as usual. Condescending. Sipping a drink, aloof from the pandemonium going on around him. Kids kicking a football up and down the passageways between tables. Babies crying. People having rows. 'I never wanted to come on this fucking holiday. It was your decision, not mine. Are you going to do something about your brats or what?'

I was always being taken to the airport to see comrades off, or meet them, but never to go anywhere myself. School journeys were always by coach. France and Spain with Councillor Nesbitt and my mother was a so-called motoring holiday.

I'd love to fly to LA or New York but my mother fucked that up for me. Instead of having my own passport when I was young, I was on Maria's. When she applied for a visa she was told,

'Ma'am, you're not a suitable person to enter the USA.'

The US State Department has a long memory. Thanks to Maria's crap I can't get a US visa either. She was ecstatic when they refused her entry into the good ol' US of A. Still talks about the threat she poses to the world's greatest-ever superpower. Ave Maria – an exile in her own country, and can't get into Babylon – always on the outside looking in. Not for me, I wanna be head first in the trough of life.

Romantic destinations are scrolling up on the monitor. Rio, Buenos Aires, Caracas, Montevideo. Chiang's been everywhere. Travelled since he was a young child of three or four which has given him an aura I'd love to acquire.

The guy with the bongs steers his luggage cart into my shins causing me to cry out in pain. Jolted out of my daydream, I hobble away swearing under my breath. *Tempus fugit* and Orson awaits. By now he must be doubting whether I'm going to show. He'll look an arsehole if I don't and I'll look an arsehole if I do.

Back where I started Orson's examining his coat buttons, flicking his cowlick and scowling. Watching me approach he consults his watch and makes hammy tsk-tsk noises. I feel as though I'm acting a part and I've got a bad case of stage fright. Concealed in the crowd is our one-man audience, Chiang.

Orson's table's cascading with used coffee cups, plastic forks and disgusting left-overs.

'You've cut it very fine,' he says. 'Let's move somewhere quieter.'

I follow him to a corner marked off for airline personnel meeting unaccompanied children. There's no one about. How will Chiang keep us in view without showing himself?

Orson's making surreal small talk. 'I'm terribly amused that Maria's daughter turned out to be the complete political opposite of her mother,' he gabbles. 'One is fascinated by the syndrome... how such offspring frequently swing the other way, Svetlana Stalin being the prime example.' The bastard's deliberately winding me up. 'Of course, it can occur in reverse,' he goes on. 'Look at old so-and-so.' He mentions an arch-Tory whose father was a Spanish Republican socialist. I want to remind him that Oswald Mosley was in the Labour Party and his son's a big-time donor, but my mouth's dry as a vulture's crotch. Where's fucking Chiang?

'All right, let's see what you've got for me,' Orson says in the weary tone of a doctor humouring a ga-ga patient.

So I produce a copy of Evelyn's taped reminiscences. Orson makes a face and tsk-tsks some more 'You expect me to listen to this now?'

'You'll just have to take my word.'

'For all I know, this could be blank.' He weighs the cassette in the palm of his manicured hand then slips it into an inside pocket.

'You know, Ms Letkin, if all the money was taken off the Channel Islands, they'd rise another six inches above sea level. They're a tax haven for nonenities who got rich by maximising their questionable talents; writers of pulp fiction, one-time pop stars; not breaking any law but tainted with a rather passé, seedy greed. I rather like their naughty but nice façade. Behind all that you have mafia money being laundered, international operators buying off-the-shelf trust companies in which to stash their fortunes. Not the sort of milieu in which one would imagine Gwendoline would survive.'

As he places a hand on my arm I draw back slightly.

'I know your mother thinks I'm a violent person, but she's wrong. There's really no need to be nervous. I wouldn't hurt a fly. Do you know why I agreed to meet you? I thought you were going to come up with the goods, Montse. I thought you were going to tell me you had conclusive proof that Gwendoline had been defrauding the ratepayers. I thought you were going to help me to put the whole matter to rest for once and for all. That's what you promised me on the telephone and that's what I expected. You've let yourself down.'

Liar!

'I thought I'd be flying off to Caracas for a break with my family secure in the knowledge that the whole nasty business was behind me.'

The F-word again!

'You know, Ms Letkin, I feel I may have triggered off Gwendoline's suicide by confronting her as I did. She was still smarting from bitter political disappointment. On top of everything, the possibility of being exposed as a larcenist may have caused her to snap. That is what I have told the police and they tend to agree with me.'

Slippery, slimy douche-bag!

'Whoops! Nearly forgot,' he feels inside his briefcase, takes out a thick manila envelope and pokes his long fingers inside. With the air of a conjuror, he slowly withdraws an airline ticket.

'For you!'

My heart leaps into my armpits, hurting me with its violent antics. My name's in red biro on the ticket.

Underneath, in the space for the destination, the same writer has spelt out in block capitals: London–Caracas.

'I went to considerable trouble to obtain that ticket, so don't disappoint me. I'm offering you a job. Courier for a world-wide business in which I have an interest. All legitimate of course. You'll travel to the kind of exotic destinations you could only dream of, the Cayman Islands, Bermuda, the Far East. The world's your oyster!'

My entire body from head to toe is slick with cowardly, shaming perspiration and my voice comes out like somebody's got me by the windpipe.

'But I haven't got my passport.'

'Oh, silly me,' he says tipping the envelope. He passes me my own fucking passport with my gormless teenage face peering up at me, pathetic virgin pages awaiting their first immigration stamps. Until this moment I had imagined that the document I am now holding in my trembling sweat-greased hands was safely locked away in a chest of drawers in my bedroom along with my misinformative birth certificate, a life-saving badge, school reports and other embarrassing juvenilia.

'Noooo!' I yell. Orson's alarmed.

'Montse, cool it. Let's talk things through.'

'You busted into my flat and you searched through my things. You scared the shit out of my flatmate. You invaded my fucking privacy!'

'Hey, don't get excited. Calm yourself.' He starts talking fast. 'OK, it was only a thought. I was trying to do you a favour. I heard you lost your job. Look, Ms Letkin, I have to go to the departure lounge. I want to pick up a few duty free things for the children. You've still got time to consider my offer. If you decide not to come out to Caracas, all well and good, if you do decide to fly out today, that's fine too. It's no big deal. How did you get out to the airport?'

I'm sitting with my elbows on my knees, my face covered with my hands making noises that mean 'no, no no!' and rocking to and fro. The ticket and passport are lying on the floor at my feet. I'm completely numb. Kind of in shock. Orson doesn't know what to do. On another level of consciousness I get satisfaction from the fact that he's flustered. An airport security geezer comes over and says, 'Everything all right, sir?'

Everything all right, *sir!* What about me? I'm the one who's in distress. Orson exudes prosperity and power. I'm a wreck. 'My daughter doesn't want to me go,' Orson says, sort of embarrassed. I wail even louder. No! The smooth way the lie drips off his lips makes me nauseous. The security man's answering voice contains no hint of doubt. He murmurs something sympathetic to Orson then moves off.

'Here,' Orson's trying to pry open my grip to force something into my fist but I'm not budging. 'Listen, my car's in the car park. Here's the ticket. Take the keys. You can use my car while I'm away.' He slips the keys into my pocket. 'I left it on the first floor, zone four.'

What's this? He's trusting me with his car. I'm wavering. Maybe Orson's for real and we've got him all wrong?

Who are our enemies, who are our friends? This is of great importance to the revolution! Maria used to sing that jingle in the bath. And I still can't work it out.

Orson lingers for a few moments longer before coolly taking his departure. Through the cracks in my fingers, his feet are walking away.

Without warning the depression about which the school psychiatrist had spoken suddenly descends. I can't move. Neither can I speak nor hear properly. My hands are stuck to my face. Through the trippy fog someone's shouting.

'Tell me, quick! Where's he going? Where's he going?'

Syllabubbles come out elongated Caar-aa-cuus. Joe

doesn't understand. I toe the airline ticket across the floor. Without a word he's grabbing the ticket like a baton in a relay race, disappearing into the thronging passengers.

Tempus fugit. How much time has passed I cannot determine. But my superhuman effort to lift my carcass and work my legs is paying off. I've forced myself to stumble over to the machine where there's a queue waiting to shove in their tickets and pay before going to their cars. My brain isn't sending any messages to my fingers. Getting the pound coins in the slot takes a while and the bastards behind me are getting ratty. What was it Orson said? First floor, zone two or second floor zone one? Every floor looks exactly the same. I'm going round in circles. There are no attendants. The system is designed to be impenetrable to foreigners. I can't crack how it works and I speak English mother tongue. How long have I been trailing back and forward? I spot Joe's car hurtling towards the exit tunnel. I have to practically fling myself into his path to make him stop.

The man's not pleased to see me. Orson didn't go to the Caracas flight and according to Joe it's all my fault.

'How was I meant to know he was lying?'

'Because he's a fucking liar, that's how!' God, I've never heard Joe swear before. I can't believe how shocked I am by his four-letter expletives. His usually gentle face is wooden. His soft eyes have hardened. He avoids looking at me. He avoids speaking to me. Just drives furiously towards the centre of town, swearing all the while. I don't even know where he's taking me.

Finally he roars up to the steps of a church near the Planetarium and stops the car. Automatically, I go to open the door and get out.

'Wait a minute! What's that ticket you're clutching?'

Trying to remember, I ogle the thing in question.

'Ticket. Car park.'

'You didn't bring your fucking car, you stupid arsehole. You came with me.'

'Orson's car.'

'What?' Joe tries to get the ticket off me but I can't let go. Orson's keys jangle in my pocket as I grapple with him.

'Leave me!'

The ticket's out of my grip and his possession. 'Zone something, level something. Take these!' I throw Orson's keys at him. We say goodbye in flat voices. I slam the door and he roars off. I see him screwing a yewie, face contorted.

By repeatedly putting one foot in front of the other, I end up near the mosque where lines of bearded men in flapping jallabeyyas are drifting through the gates. Without a sense of direction or time, none of this has anything to do with me. Why not move to a different town, leave everything behind? Who would notice or care? But I've lived in this city all my life and I've got a right to be here. This is where I went to nursery school when I was a few months old. School, health clinic. All my old haunts. What would I get for my flat? The mortgage is only two years old. The value of the place hasn't had a chance to rise. I'd lose out badly on the deal if I bought anything else and I'd have no chance of getting social housing or housing benefit. Even if I had a baby, which I wouldn't, I'm just saying *if*, I'd have to spend years in a shit hole like Widdecombe Hall.

Why did I let Joe make me feel as if the whole plan had failed because of me? It was his idea to entrap Orson. Not mine. If I'd gone to Maria and consulted her, we might have come up with a more subtle plan, one which might have had a chance of success. I have complete faith in Maria's ability to make infallible plans, despite the fact that she got herself into some hairy situations in the past. The point is she learned from them. Tactically, she's equivalent to a military genius conducting a cunning guerilla war against a more powerful enemy. Surrounding the cities from the countryside. Or that's how I see her; a military tactician or chess player, outwitting the professionals and undermining the power structures, keeping alive a tradition which it was hoped had been buried in the post-this and that millennium.

Envy overwhelms me when I think of my mother, I feel a kind of madness based on jealousy. Maria has proved herself over and over; emerged victorious from countless battles with authority, overcome bad relationships with men and always refused to accept the definitions imposed by society.

Still wandering through the streets. Hungrily searching for the right kind of caff. One which serves real coffee, Italian sandwiches and also accepts plastic.

On entering, this place appeared exactly right but the coffee's bitter, the food tasteless and dry. Toilet's down grimy stairs. And I glimpse a salmonella-friendly kitchen, chef yelling at a fellow worker in Serbo-Croat. The food doesn't satisfy me, but at least I've filled my stomach and emptied my bladder. Paying by plastic, I'm ignoring the portion on my bill which the sullen waiter has left blank for me to add a tip, pressing the ball point firmly into the tablecloth to make sure the imprint penetrates all the copies as the man stands over me.

Back in my flat, I'm impelled to brush my teeth vigorously to rid my mouth of the sickly after-effects of mozzarella, before going to the fridge and opening a can of fresh-tasting beer.

Exhaustion keeps me awake, seething in my head. Not sure I was right to turn down Orson's offer of a job. I might have blown my only chance to join the beautiful people. After the débâcle at the airport I'm completely beaten. My efforts to redeem myself have failed. From now on I will not venture out. I will render myself unconscious.

I ring the local offie and order a couple of dozen bottles of plonk and a few boxes of tortilla chips. The manager repeats my order in a knowing drawl. So I add on a bottle of Southern Comfort and a litre of Absolut to shut him up. That should take away the pain!

All this is more than the groping mistakes of youth. I hate to think how I've frittered away the last few years, pinning everything on false aspirations, trusting the wrong people, believing in the wrong axioms and current catch-phrases and short cuts to success. Then experiencing let down and betrayal; feeling used by people but not quite knowing whether that is the case or not. I've got a fatal weakness when it comes to making up my own mind about things, I end up trying to conceal my lack of confidence with clownish brash behaviour. Drunkenness. Over eagerness to please Joe. Then hating him.

Everything's fucked up just when my problems seemed to be sorting out. Suspension from my job, the Cheeseface denunciation and now the bungled airport scenario.

Hey, I'm beginning to see where I'm going wrong! Up till now I haven't fully grasped that what I need to do is stop doing what I do, instead of doing it more. Instead of one last spectacular piece of snooping to impress everyone, stop doing what I'm doing. Do nothing and see what happens.

The pleasant tinkle of bottles rattling in a crate is rising up my stairs. Whoosh! A controlled crash and the crate is deposited outside my door. The delivery person clatters my letterbox as if they haven't already got my full attention.

'Just leave it there,' I yell through the aperture at the guy's belt buckle. When he's gone I drag the cardboard box filled with blood red wine into my own space. Let the party commence!

Drinking to lose consciousness is one thing, staying unconscious is something else. I go in and out, dreaming of falling, crashing and smashing. Next minute I'm naked in a supermarket, running up and down between the aisles, waking up drenched in sweat. Now someone I love is being incarcerated in a bin. In my dreams I have feelings of love towards people. In real life, I don't. She's in a wheelchair. Her face lights up as she tells me. At last they believe her. She isn't crazy and they're going to let her out. We're elated. At that moment I have a very strong urge to pee. I go off to find a toilet. When I come back she's gone. No one will tell me where she is. They pretend she doesn't exist. Is she Weezie? Is she Maria? I don't remember. Then I'm the one who's being incarcerated in the bin and my loved one's trying to talk the authorities into letting me go free. They won't listen.

Wetness in the small of my back may be part of the dream or perhaps exists in reality. I haven't got the strength to check if I've peed the bed. Voices and banging. Orson, decked out in Nazi uniform, is pulling my teeth with a large pair of callipers. My dream is now taking place through a pin-hole. A man deported to Buchenwald from Guernsey made himself a pin-hole camera and took pictures inside the camp. I saw them in the paper. A man who stayed on Guernsey painted a Union Jack on his wall then papered over it. Only he knows that it is there. I see him genuflucting to the wall in his small, freshly papered, front room. Smell the wallpaper paste. Outside, he smartly salutes the Nazi soldiers.

The door's booted in. I'm back in the squat with my mother. She's reciting in her Rosie the Riveter voice from a little red book. *A frog in a well says, 'The sky is no bigger than the mouth of the well.'*

Drifting through a tunnel. Voices and banging again. Orson's stuffing something down my throat and I'm floating above the scene as my body is hoisted onto a gurney and trundled out of the flat.

endings

CURLED UP IN THE bottom of a coracle with my knees up under my chin. Rolling. Lifted by waves and sinking, sickeningly. Choking. Muddle-headed. Voices calling my name. My guts sucking out through a tube which is inserted in my throat, scraping my mucous membranes. Am I in hospital? Visiting my mother? Can't be that. This time I'm the one in the bed.

Nobody hears my screams. They're pumping my stomach out of spite. I didn't take many pills. A burly copper wearing full body armour and a side-handle baton guards my door.

'When can we talk to her?' a nasal voice nags. Doctors murmur, 'She's coming round. Won't be long.'

Surely my head's been decapitated and stuck back on with a tubigrip. I want to throw up but there's nothing inside.

'We found the car, Montse,' the smug nasal voice says. 'And we found what Orson left for us in the boot. A certain trade unionist with a few members missing, so to speak. Are you with us, Montse?'

Can't even shake my head in case it falls off. Funny thing is, I couldn't give Jack Shit.

All I want is to sink into the deepest possible slumber. The nasal one has gone and someone else has taken his place at my bedside. Hughie in counselling mode. Unbeknown to me Maureen had been worrying. When Hughie arrived at the town hall looking for me she was relieved of the responsibility of being the only person who was worried.

'She knew your address but she wouldn't turn up out of the blue. Not ordinarily, without an invite,' Hughie says. 'But she saw it more in the line of a professional visit. It was brilliant the way she got your door open.'

He's convinced that owing to my temporary abstention from life, I'm interested in developments. I couldn't care less but he's going to tell me anyway. How Stan's body was found in the boot of Orson's car at the airport. Hughie holds up a newspaper. *Trade Unionist Battered to Death*. Stan's in the paper, smiling outside Congress House, wearing the lethal lime green jacket. I could have driven that car home and never known his body was in the boot till the pong raised the alarm. Or, it could have been me in the boot!

'It's all over, Montse. You don't have to worry about anything. A cop working under cover at the airport got on to Interpol and Orson was arrested at Madrid Airport. Murder. Embezzlement. The story was big on the 10 o'clock news. Orson even had a bunch of senior policemen in his pocket. This young detective's blown the whistle on the lot of them. They're all pointing the finger at each other. Orson'll be going down for a long, long time.'

I don't suppose I'll ever know for sure what Joe's strategy was towards me. I think he just uses intuition, flattery and lies to get whatever he wants from people; in my case he got information and a patsy to front up to Orson. My involvement may have made no difference in the end, or it may have been crucial. I don't care. I've given it all up. Let it go. From now on I'm chucking up the dirty work, especially other people's.

Hughie says, 'Maria doesn't care what you do so long as you're clean-hearted.'

Couldn't care less. Only want to be left alone.

Hughie tries to interest me in his own story. And, unexpectedly, I find myself listening. A couple of years ago he looked after his dying lover and did lots of counselling at an Aids organisation. He still isn't ready for a sexual partnership but he found a soulmate in Maria and was happy to commit himself to helping her over her operation.

'I was in the habit of being a carer,' he says. Some people have strange habits! Says he was aware caring was a habit but he's not addicted to it.

Hughie and Maria met at a community housing conference attended by the sort of people I may have been keeping tabs on when I was following orders.

No more denial. No more pretending what I did wasn't so bad.

'Maria told me something about your father that I think you should know,' Hughie says. 'Maybe this isn't a good time, but I think you've been kept in ignorance long enough. Do you want me to go on?'

My eyes meet his and I'm trying to say yes.

In the sixties and early seventies my mother belonged to a variety of self-proclaimed left-wing groups. Sexual liberation was interpreted as men fucking anything that moved and women's position was prone except when they were cooking, or making tea for the comrades. One-night stands were compulsory in many such communes.

'In one group, Maria was forbidden to sleep with the

same man for two nights running,' Hughie tells me. Why change the habits of a lifetime?

Around the time of Nixon's Christmas bombing, I was conceived. Nixon's Christmas bombing? The phrase hangs together in the same way as Stratchey's ground nuts. 'Cambodia,' Hughie explains, 'Nixon's Christmas bombing of Cambodia.' So Pol Pot cannot lay claim to all the bones littering the killing fields. Uncle Sam, another psychopathic loner, must own his share.

A new man had joined the group. Adolpho from Colombia. A man with romantic, revolutionary looks. A Pancho Gonzales moustache. A dedicated man. A man who took copious notes at study sessions, was first to step forward for any task, turning the handle on the Gestetner machine while my mother typed out leaflets, carrying one side of the banner while my mother carried the other. A man who, besides the works of Mao, Franz Fanon and General Giap, read *Revolt on the Clyde*, *Red Star over China*, and *The Autobiography of Malcolm X*. An irresistible man. In short, the man my mother had been waiting for all her life. Or, to be precise, since sentient life began, which she dated from the time she heard Stokely Carmichael berating a crowd of guilty white liberals at the Round House circa 1967.

Hughie goes on relentlessly.

'When your mother refused to carry on as part of the musical beds arrangement, the other men were annoyed. Said she'd fallen prey to the sugar-coated bullets of the bourgeoisie.

'Rumours began spreading among comrades that the man wasn't all he pretended to be. A few things didn't add up. For example, he'd go missing for a day or two here, a day or two there and he always drove a different car. "I work for Godfrey Davis and it's my job to deliver cars," he said. That satisfied them temporarily.

'He also claimed to work at a club called the Tatty Bogle. When the comrades went down to check on his story, the Tatty Bogle had never heard of him. Still Maria refused to believe he was Scotland Yard.

'Then, at a meeting at the LSE, attended by lots of different groups who were getting together to oppose the carnage in Indo-China, he was recognised by a cadre from a Trotskyite group. By chance one of their members lived in a block of flats where it was common knowledge that the apartment below was occupied by a mixed group of women and men who worked for Scotland Yard.

'At first, Maria refused to believe he was a police spy. She went on stubbornly protesting that you couldn't trust a Trot and the accusation had only been made to sabotage the Maoists. But immediately after Adolpho was pointed out at the meeting he just disappeared. His cover was blown. He walked out of the meeting. Never to be seen again.'

Adolpho? What kind of people would call their kid Adolpho in the 1940s? No wonder Mum was so gutted when she heard about my wonderful job.

'You all right, Montse?'

'Couldn't care less, Hughie. I just want to be left alone.'

'To do what?'

'None of your business.'

Actually I want to think about my Mum, Ave Maria, what she'd been through. All that crap, years, no, decades of it, and she waded through it like one of those heroic night soil workers in the revolting little ditty she used to sing instead of a namby-pamby loola-loola-loola-loola-loo lullaby when I was in my diapers. And keeping to her principles all the time, despite the vagaries of political fashion. It's always been a mystery to me, right, but now it hits me, where she's at.

Shock! Tears are flowing. I actually feel like seeing the old girl. What have they given me in here?

Squealing of tyres on lino. Turning my head, squinting into strip lighting, I think I see her! Coming through the door. Is she sitting? Her shoulders and arms are gyrating. Propelling herself, wheeling up to me.

'Where'd you nick the chair?'
'Physio.'
I reach out the side of the bed and grab her hand.
'Awright, Montse?'
'Yeah. You?'

Also by Diane Langford and published by Serpent's Tail

Shame About the Street

'Wicked and funny' ***Pink Paper***

'A right-on slice of dystopian paranoia' ***The Herald***

'There in the paper was a photograph of the newsreader in a fashionable restaurant, leaning across the table towards a companion whose face was in the shadow. Their hands were touching. A white circle was superimposed around the head of the other woman whose face was invisible.'

A boiling summer day in the not-too-distant future in London, and business goes on despite the stifling heat: the tabloid newspapers churn out lurid headlines, cleaners in the newspaper offices go to work, and at Victoria station, Rosemary, a civil servant, is on her way to work. Rich, demure, and dull, Rosemary is the ideal Home Counties Woman and government cog in the wheels. But before the end of the day she will become 'The Lesbian Civil Servant' exposed by tabloids as the leak on the government's proposed re-introduction of an Anti-Homosexual law.

Shame About the Street is a bitter-sweet investigation into the mores of the press and society of today.

Also published by Serpent's Tail

Stella Duffy

Beneath the Blonde

Siobhan Forrester, lead singer of Beneath the Blonde, has everything a girl could want – stunning body, great voice, brilliant career, loving boyfriend. Now she has a stalker too. She can cope with the midnight flower deliveries and nasty phone calls, but things really turn sour when intimidation turns to murder.

Saz Martin, hired to seek out the stalker and protect Siobhan, embarks on a whirlwind investigation, travelling with the band from London to New Zealand, via the rest of the world. As jobs go, this one shouldn't be too hard, except Siobhan isn't telling the whole truth and Saz isn't sure she wants to keep the relationship strictly business.

Beneath the Blonde is the third Saz Martin thriller, following the highly acclaimed **Calendar Girl** and **Wavewalker**, and confirming Stella Duffy's position at the forefront of the new wave of British crime fiction.

'Saz Martin is ... an ebullient heroine of courage and wry wit ... Duffy's third novel removes her from the category of "promising" and confirms without doubt that she's very near the top of the new generation of modern crime writers.' **Marcel Berlins** *The Times*

'Stella Duffy's writing gets better with each book.' **Val McDermid** *Manchester Evening News*

'Always a pleasure to find a new Stella Duffy novel ... a good read and highly recommended' *Diva*

Agnes Bushell

The Enumerator

Lamont Bliss came to San Francisco all right, but when they found him dead the flowers he wore weren't just in his hair – they were spilling out of every wound in his mutilated body.

What happened to Lamont should never have been any of Alex's business. She was just back from New Mexico and the main thing on her mind was choosing a new tattoo. Then Sean the enumerator came calling.

The enumerators were everywhere that year, sex surveyors tracking the spread of HIV in San Francisco. But when someone told the enumerator a little too much about their sex life – that's when the killing started.

Driven by passion and violence, soaked in fear and sex, **The Enumerator** offers the sharpest take on San Francisco since Dashiell Hammett's **Maltese Falcon**.

'Bushell's post-AIDS, alternative San Francisco – a rich stew of blood lust, hypocrisy and death, Star Trek re-runs, queer outings, and a promise of love – proves as arresting as her tattooed heroine's foreground investigation into a gay murder imaginatively executed – corpse as floral display.' *Guardian*

'A twisting, subtle thriller of San Francisco in the AIDS years. Bushell conveys wonderfully well the lurking anger and darkness beneath this most sophisticated of American cities.' *GQ*

Charlotte Carter

Rhode Island Red

Street saxophonist and Grace Jones lookalike Nannette has a masters in French, an on-off boyfriend called Walter and a dead undercover cop in her apartment. But her life starts getting really complicated when she discovers $60,000 stuffed into her sax, the cop's ex-colleagues turn up and she's courted by that elegant older man who wants her to teach him everything she knows about Charlie Parker.
And who, or what is Rhode Island Red?

'Elegiac and musical .. Nan is a wonderful character' **Liza Cody**

'Wholly delightful ... the year's freshest crime debut' ***GQ***

'Sharp, funny and beautifully underscored with jazzy prose riffs' ***Good Housekeeping***

'Irresistible New York fable ... sex and jokes and a love for jazz which blows hot, cool and true from beginning to end' ***Literary Review***

'It's refreshing to find a heroine who has both a rock-solid moral centre and a sense of humour' ***Sunday Times***

'Enough spirit to keep you turning till the final page' ***The Voice***